THE BOBBSEY TWINS
MYSTERY AT SCHOOL

"There goes someone!" Flossie shouted

The Bobbsey Twins' Mystery at School

BY
LAURA LEE HOPE

GROSSET & DUNLAP
Publishers • New York

Published in 2004 by Grosset & Dunlap, a division of Penguin Young
Readers Group, 345 Hudson Street, New York, New York 10014.
GROSSET & DUNLAP is a trademark of Penguin Group (USA) Inc.
THE BOBBSEY TWINS® is a registered trademark of
Simon & Schuster, Inc.

Printed in the U.S.A.

ISBN 0-448-43755-4

3 5 7 9 10 8 6 4 2

CONTENTS

CHAPTER 1

THE CIRCUS TRAIN

"OOH! Look at the dog!" blond Flossie Bobbsey cried. "He's doing tricks!"

"Yes, and he's really good!" said Nan, who was Flossie's twelve-year-old sister.

The two girls stood on the platform of the Ocean Cliff station. Far down at the end they could see a man and a white dog. The dog jumped back and forth across the man's outstretched arm, then pranced around him on his hind legs.

"What are you looking at?" The question came from a little boy of six who had just run out of the waiting room. He was Freddie Bobbsey, Flossie's twin brother.

As the girls pointed to the performing dog, they were joined by Bert, who was Nan's twin, and Dorothy Minturn, the Bobbseys' cousin.

Bert's brown eyes flashed with excitement.

1

"The stationmaster just told us that train over on the siding has a circus on board. They stopped here to take on water for the animals."

"Animals!" Freddie shouted. "Let's go see them!"

"May we, Mommy?" Flossie asked a slim, pretty woman who stood by a pile of luggage.

Mrs. Bobbsey turned away from her sister, Dorothy's mother. The Bobbsey family had been spending a vacation with the Minturns at their seashore home.

"I think you'd better stay here," Mrs. Bobbsey replied. "Our train to Lakeport is due very soon."

"Oh, okay," Flossie agreed, "I wouldn't want to miss it 'cause I can hardly wait to see Daddy!"

"Me too!" echoed Freddie, "and I want to see Snoop!"

"And how about Dinah?" Nan asked with a smile.

Snoop was the Bobbseys' black cat and Dinah was the jolly colored woman who helped Mrs. Bobbsey with the housework. Dinah and her husband Sam, who worked for Mr. Bobbsey at his lumberyard, lived in an apartment on the third floor of the Bobbsey house in Lakeport.

"It'll be great to see them all!" Bert spoke up for the small twins.

Nan looked down the platform again. "The dog is gone!" she exclaimed in disappointment.

"Maybe he belongs to the circus," Dorothy suggested. "That man might just have been exercising him."

The children eyed the circus train curiously. Suddenly Flossie poked Freddie. "Look!" she cried.

Stepping from the last car of the train was the tallest man any of them had ever seen. He was also very thin. His suit of blue and white stripes made him look even taller and thinner.

"And look who's coming next!" Dorothy giggled as the tall man turned to help a woman down the steps.

"The big lady!" Flossie exclaimed with a gasp.

The woman was almost as wide as she was tall. She was too broad for the narrow passage and had to come down the steps sideways. Once down she tucked her hand under the tall man's arm, and they began to pace back and forth beside the train.

"You'll be that big, Flossie, if you keep on eating so much ice cream!" Bert said teasingly.

Flossie made a face at her brother, and Freddie chuckled.

"They're coming this way," Nan observed a moment later.

The children watched as the odd pair walked up the platform. When they reached the station the tall man said something to the big lady and went into the waiting room.

His companion stood by the door swinging a small handbag. Suddenly it dropped from her hand. The big lady made an attempt to bend down, but she was too large. Her arms could not reach the bag.

"I'll get it for you!" Freddie called. He dashed over and picked up the purse and gave it to the woman.

The big lady beamed. "Thank you, little boy," she said. "I haven't been able to reach the ground for years. If I could do that, I'd lose my job with the circus!" She shook with merry laughter.

At that moment the engine whistle gave three loud blasts. The tall man hurried out of the waiting room, and he and the big lady moved off toward the waiting train.

"Hank!" the children heard the thin man call.

Another man appeared at the top of the steps and held his hands down toward the big lady. She grasped them and with assistance from the tall man managed to heave herself up the steps. The thin man climbed up and, stooping, followed her into the car.

There were sounds of doors slamming. The train slowly pulled back onto the main track and gathered speed. Soon it disappeared in the distance.

"I wish we could have seen the animals," Freddie remarked wistfully.

Aunt Emily Minturn looked up at the sky. "It looks as if we're going to have a storm. Maybe Hurricane Betsy is coming this way."

"Who is Hurricane Betsy?" Flossie asked. "Will we be able to see her?"

Mrs. Bobbsey explained that Betsy was the name which the Weather Bureau had given to this particular tropical storm.

"Oh!" said Flossie in disappointment. "I thought she was a little girl."

"Here comes our train!" Bert called out. He began to help the porter gather up the luggage.

In another minute the train came to a halt in front of the group. A conductor swung to the ground. "All aboard!" he shouted.

There was much laughter and confusion as the Bobbseys said good-by to the Minturns and thanked them for the pleasant visit. The twins stood on the platform for a last wave to Dorothy as the train pulled out of the station.

The porter and Bert piled the luggage in a space at the end of the car. Then the children went to their seats, and the conductor closed the door.

"Looks like we're going to have a taste of Betsy!" he said as he took the tickets from Mrs. Bobbsey. She sat opposite Freddie and Flossie in facing seats. Nan and Bert were across the aisle.

Freddie giggled. "Will she taste good?"

The conductor laughed. "I don't know about Betsy. She's a very changeable young lady. She was supposed to go out to sea, but she's turned back to land!"

"I'm not afraid of a storm named Betsy!" Freddie announced stoutly. "Girls can't hurt you!"

"That's right, young fellow!" the conductor said with a twinkle in his eyes. "Anyway, you'll be perfectly safe on the train."

The kindly man went on, and the children settled down in their seats. Freddie and Flossie began to put a puzzle together while Bert and Nan took out books.

Everything was quiet until Flossie became restless. "I'm going to practice writing," she decided. She leaned over to Bert in the next seat. "Do you have a pencil?"

Bert put his hand into his pocket. Then he exclaimed. "The letter! I forgot it!"

"What letter?" Nan asked curiously.

"Just as we left Aunt Emily's the mailman gave me a letter. I put it in my pocket and forgot all about it!" Bert pulled out the envelope and studied it. "It's from Mr. Tetlow," he said in surprise. Mr. Tetlow was the tall, gray-haired principal of the Bobbseys' school.

"Maybe you've been expelled!" Nan teased.

"Read it! Quick!" Flossie said impatiently.

Bert tore open the envelope and read the letter. "Say, this is great!" he exclaimed.

"What is it, Bert? Tell us," Nan pleaded.

Mrs. Bobbsey smiled. "Yes, we're all interested," she said.

Bert quickly read the letter once more. Then he explained that Mr. Tetlow was planning to start a small museum at the school. The principal felt it would help in the history and geography classes. He had already secured some articles which had been loaned for the first exhibits.

"But why did he write to you?" Nan asked, puzzled.

"Well, he wants as many children as possible to contribute something to put on display. And he has asked me to be head of the museum committee."

"I think that's a great honor, Bert," Mrs. Bobbsey spoke up. "I'm sure you'll do a good job."

The other children excitedly congratulated their brother. Then, after discussing the museum for a while longer, they turned back to what they had been doing.

Shortly afterwards Nan looked up from her book with a puzzled expression. "The light is so faint that I can hardly read," she said.

"No wonder," Bert replied. "Look outside!"

The Bobbseys peered from the windows. Black clouds scudded across a gray sky. The wind blew furiously and made the branches of the trees twist and toss in a wild sort of dance.

Horses and cows huddled in little groups near a fence or under a tree. Once in a while a man could be seen dashing across a field fighting his way against the wind.

"Is this Betsy?" Flossie asked her mother anxiously.

"I'm afraid it is, and the storm seems to be getting worse," Mrs. Bobbsey replied.

As she spoke the train was running past a meadow in the center of which was a clump of tall trees.

"Look!" Nan cried.

The tallest of the trees seemed to shiver for a minute, then it crashed to the ground, the great mound of roots pulling out of the earth.

"And see that roof!" Freddie called out.

As if some giant hand had lifted it, a barn roof rose into the air and sailed off with the wind. A moment later it landed in the middle of a cornfield.

It had started to rain. Now the water came down in great sheets. It beat against the train windows and streamed down so heavily that it was impossible to look out.

"Ooh!" Flossie cried. "How can the man see to run the train?"

"It's on a track, silly," Freddie said. "He doesn't have to see."

The train sped on through the storm. Suddenly the pace slowed, and the engine seemed to be almost crawling along. The conductor walked back through the car, an expression of concern on his face.

"Why have we slowed down?" Bert asked when the man came near him.

The conductor stopped. "Everything's all right," he assured the boy. "We're coming near High Point trestle. The engineer is going over very slowly in case the structure has been weakened by the storm."

Now the wind sent the rain against the windows in sudden gusts. One minute the panes would be clear and the next covered with water. The train crept on.

Shading her eyes with her hands, Nan gazed through the glass. The train was on the trestle now. Far, far down she could see a muddy river racing along between low banks.

Just then Flossie cried out, "Oh, Mommy, the train's wobbling!"

CHAPTER II

A FREE PERFORMANCE

THE other twins waited breathlessly to see what the train would do.

"The wind's blowing it," said Mrs. Bobbsey. "But don't worry about our falling into the water. We're already across the trestle."

The children heaved sighs of relief as the train gathered speed once more. Gradually the rain slackened, and finally it stopped altogether. The wind died down. An hour later the conductor came through the car. This time he had a cheerful smile.

"We've left Betsy behind us!" he told the Bobbseys. "We got just the fringe of the storm. The weather is clearing ahead."

"How soon will we be in Lakeport?" Bert asked.

The conductor looked at his watch. "The engineer is making up time now," he said. "We should be in Lakeport in about twenty minutes!"

As he spoke, there was a screeching, grinding sound. The train jerked to a stop with such a jolt that all the passengers were thrown forward in their seats. The conductor kept his balance by grabbing the back of Bert's seat. Then before anyone could ask him a question he dashed from the car.

"I wonder what happened?" Nan said, peering from the window.

"It's a wreck!" one of the women passengers cried excitedly.

"We must be off the track!" a man exclaimed.

The Bobbsey twins were always surrounded by excitement of some sort. In an *Adventure in the Country* they had caught the thief who had stolen their cousin Harry's prize bull. They found *The Secret at the Seashore* in a message in a bottle and helped to rescue a little girl's father.

The friendly conductor returned. "Nothing to worry about, folks!" he announced. "The circus train running ahead of us hit a large tree that the wind had blown across the tracks."

"Was anyone hurt?" Mrs. Bobbsey asked anxiously.

The conductor explained that the first two cars of the circus train had been derailed, but no one was injured. "Our engineer had to stop suddenly to avoid running into the back of the other train."

Flossie jumped back as something tapped on the window beside her. "What's that?" she squealed.

"A monkey!" Freddie shouted.

The little animal, who looked like a bald old man wearing spectacles, sat on the outside of the window sill. When Freddie put his face close to the window, the monkey stuck out his tongue.

Nan laughed. "I don't think he likes you, Freddie!" she said.

"It's just because he doesn't know me," her small brother answered quickly.

"Did the monkey come from the circus train?" Bert asked.

"Yes. The first car held the monkeys and dogs," the conductor told them. "There were ponies in the second one. They all got loose when the cars went off the track. The guards are having a hard time rounding them up."

"Aren't there any bears and tigers?" Freddie asked.

"They are in the other cars and didn't get out."

"Thank goodness!" Mrs. Bobbsey said. "I'm glad there aren't any wild animals wandering around!"

Monkeys were swinging from the branches
of nearby trees

"Let's go watch the circus people catch the monkeys," Bert proposed.

Mrs. Bobbsey agreed and the twins hurried off the train. A strange sight met their eyes. Monkeys were scampering over the tops of the cars and swinging from the branches of nearby trees.

Several gray French poodles ran up and down beside the track barking frantically. In a field six white ponies galloped around excitedly.

Circus attendants raced to and fro trying to catch the various animals. Suddenly something landed on Nan's shoulder. It was the bald-headed monkey they had seen on the window sill!

Nan took the little animal in her arms. He clung to her, shivering and chattering.

"The poor thing's frightened!" Nan cried. She began to smooth his fur.

At that moment one of the ponies left the field and ran past the children. Quick as a flash, the monkey jumped from Nan's arms and landed on the pony's back. There he perched as the pony turned and trotted back toward the field.

"Wasn't that funny?" Flossie asked in delight.

"It's probably the monkey's act in the circus —riding on the pony," Bert remarked.

A woman's voice called out, "In the ring, Prince!"

Obediently the pony joined the others in the field. A young woman walked over carrying a long whip. At a crack of the whip the six ponies began to trot around in a circle. Then as the children watched, monkeys dropped from the trees. In a few minutes a monkey was riding on the back of each white pony!

"Isn't this 'citing?" Flossie exclaimed.

"It sure is," Bert agreed. "We're having a private circus performance!"

"I wonder where the fat lady and the tall man are?" Nan said. Many of the circus people were standing about, but there was no sign of the two they had seen on the Ocean Cliff platform.

"I guess maybe the fat lady's stuck in her seat!" Flossie said with a giggle, "and the tall man is trying to pull her out!"

Another crack of the young woman's whip had sent the ponies out of the field and up a ramp into the second railroad car. By this time the rest of the monkeys and the poodles had been caught and were back on the train. The twins returned to their seats.

"Can the men put the circus train back on the

tracks?" Freddie asked after they had told their mother about the animals.

"I don't know," Mrs. Bobbsey replied. "We'll ask the conductor when he comes through again."

When the question was put to the man a few minutes later, he shook his head. "I'm afraid it will take several hours to clear the track," he replied. "I suggest that any passengers who wish to, walk across the field to the highway. It isn't far, and the railroad company will send out buses to take you into Lakeport."

"Let's do that, Mother," Freddie urged. "I'm tired of sitting in this train!"

"All right," Mrs. Bobbsey agreed. "We'll leave the large suitcases to be put off at Lakeport and carry the small ones."

Bert and Nan each picked up an overnight bag. Freddie flung the coats over his shoulder.

"I'll take Linda's suitcase," Flossie said. Linda was her favorite doll and had been with her both at the seashore and in the country.

As the little girl stood up on the train seat and pulled the doll's suitcase from the luggage rack, the clasp opened. Out onto the seat and floor of the aisle spilled the doll clothes, as well as some shells which Flossie had picked up on the beach. Several of the shells broke.

"Oh dear!" Flossie cried.

"Never mind," said Nan. "We'll write to Dorothy and ask her to send some more shells."

She and Flossie scrambled around the floor and in a minute had all the clothes and shells back in the suitcase again.

By this time the other passengers had left the car. The Bobbseys were the last to come down the train steps. They said good-by to the friendly conductor, who promised to see that their luggage was put off at Lakeport.

"Ooh, it's dark!" Flossie exclaimed as she jumped to the ground and followed her mother. It was true. Dusk had fallen.

"There's a path here which must lead to the highway," Mrs. Bobbsey pointed out. "I'll go first. You and Freddie come after me. Bert and Nan will walk last."

The procession started off across the field. The path was hard to follow in the darkness, and the other people from the train were far ahead.

Flossie stumbled over a stone and fell. Mrs. Bobbsey helped her up. "Perhaps you'd better hold Freddie's hand, dear," her mother suggested.

"All right," Flossie agreed.

"Are you sure we're going toward the highway?" Nan called. "I don't see any lights."

"I think there's a patch of woods ahead. The road is on the other side of that," Mrs. Bobbsey replied.

They walked on in silence for a few minutes. Then Bert, who brought up the rear, whispered to Nan, "Do you hear something behind us?"

"No. What do you mean?" his twin asked.

"Something has been following us," Bert said in a low tone. "It sounds more like an animal than a person—maybe one of the escaped circus animals."

"Don't say anything about it," Nan warned. "You'll frighten Freddie and Flossie!"

She hurried to catch up to the others, but Bert's remark had made her more aware of strange sounds. "There *is* something back there!" she decided with a little shiver.

By this time the sound had become louder. There was a steady *pit-pat, pit-pat* of footsteps on the hard ground.

Mrs. Bobbsey stopped, and the twins gathered around her. "Is someone following us?" she asked.

"Yes," Bert replied. "I've been hearing the footsteps for some time, but I didn't want to worry you."

"Maybe it's a tiger!" Freddie cried.

CHAPTER III

A LOST DOG

NAN laughed nervously. "I'm sure it's not a tiger, Freddie," she said. "Remember, the conductor said the car the wild animals were in hadn't left the track!"

"One might have 'scaped!" Freddie insisted.

"Come on, children," Mrs. Bobbsey said firmly. "I'm sure there's nothing dangerous back of us, and we must hurry on to the highway before it gets any darker."

They walked as fast as they could. Mrs. Bobbsey led the way while Nan held Flossie's hand and Bert took Freddie's. Still the *pit-pat* behind them grew louder.

Just then the moon broke through the clouds. At the same moment they heard a friendly bark.

"It's a dog!" Bert cried, beginning to laugh.

The twins and their mother turned in the path. Bounding toward them was a large, white, shaggy dog. He wagged his tail in greeting.

"Oh, isn't he nice!" Nan exclaimed. "I wonder where he came from?"

"Here, boy!" Bert snapped his fingers.

Instantly the dog stood up on his hind legs and began to march around in a circle.

"What a funny doggie!" Flossie cried, clapping her hands.

At the sound the dog dropped to all fours again and ran over to the little girl. He stood in front of her, fluffy tail waving and his tongue hanging out.

"He's smiling at me!" Flossie exclaimed in delight. She leaned over and patted him.

At that the dog sat down and held out one paw. "Shake hands with him, Flossie!" Freddie urged.

When the children had each shaken the dog's paw, Mrs. Bobbsey spoke up. "He's certainly a well-trained dog, but don't play with him any more. We don't want him to follow us. His owner wouldn't like it."

"I wish he was ours!" Freddie said wistfully.

"Remember, you have Snoop," his mother replied. "You wouldn't want both a dog *and* a cat!"

"Sure I would!" Freddie persisted.

At Mrs. Bobbsey's urging the twins resumed their walk to the highway. The dog sat down and looked after them. Flossie turned and waved to him.

They had gone only a little way when Nan called out, "The dog is still following us!"

Mrs. Bobbsey glanced back. The big white

dog was padding after them, wagging his tail.

"Go back! Go home!" Mrs. Bobbsey called sternly.

The dog stopped. He lay down in the path, his head between his forepaws, his eyes looking up at them mournfully.

"He wants to come with us," Flossie said. "Maybe he doesn't belong to anyone!"

"A trained dog like that must have a master," her mother observed. "Come on, we're almost at the highway."

"Perhaps the dog is the one we saw doing tricks on the platform at Ocean Cliff," Nan suggested after a few minutes. "He may belong to the circus."

"That dog wasn't so big as this one," Flossie stated positively.

The Bobbseys walked on, and in a short while came to the highway. Parked at the side of the road was a station wagon and a truck.

"There's Daddy!" Flossie shrieked, running up to a tall handsome man who had just stepped from the station wagon.

"How's my little sweet fairy?" he teased as he picked Flossie up and swung her into the air. This was Mr. Bobbsey's favorite nickname for his younger daughter. He called Freddie his fireman because the little boy loved to play with toy fire engines and said he was going to be a fireman when he grew up.

"Dick!" Mrs. Bobbsey exclaimed. "How do you happen to be here?"

"Sam and I went to the Lakeport station to meet you. When we heard that the track was blocked, we decided to try picking you up here."

He explained that Sam had put some benches in the truck so that he could take passengers into town if they wished to go. Although the railroad had sent several buses, there was not room for all the people from the train and the lumberyard truck was already full of passengers. At a signal from Mr. Bobbsey, Sam drove off.

"We've had a very 'citing time!" Flossie explained. "We saw the monkeys ride on the ponies."

"And one monkey made a face at me!" Freddie chuckled.

"Where did that dog come from?" Mr. Bobbsey asked, pointing behind the twins.

The children whirled. The white dog had caught up to them and now stood wagging his tail so hard it seemed as if it would shake right off!

Bert explained about hearing the animal following them and said they had thought perhaps it was a wild animal escaped from the circus train. "And it turned out to be this dog!" he ended with a grin.

"May we take him home with us, please, Daddy?" Flossie pleaded.

"But doesn't he belong to somebody?" Mr. Bobbsey asked in surprise.

"We don't know," Bert admitted. "But he might be run over if we leave him here on the highway."

Mr. Bobbsey walked over and examined the dog's neck. "He doesn't have a collar or a license," he observed. "We might take him along until we can find out where he belongs."

"Goody! Goody!" Flossie cried. She and Freddie climbed into the third seat of the station wagon. The dog jumped up and settled down between them.

For the first part of the ride to Lakeport the twins were busy telling their father about the past few days at Ocean Cliff and about Hurricane Betsy.

But after a little while there was silence in the back seat. Bert turned around, then motioned the others to look. Freddie and Flossie were sound asleep, their heads on the shaggy back of the big white dog!

A few minutes later, they awoke when Mr. Bobbsey pulled into the driveway of the Bobbseys' rambling white house. The door flew open, and Dinah hurried out.

"I'm right glad to see you!" the cook called as she began to help take the bags out of the station wagon. "And I've got a nice supper all ready for you!"

"That sounds good, Dinah," Bert said as he helped his mother from the car.

"My lands!" Dinah threw up her hands in surprise. "What's that you all have in there?"

"A dog!" Freddie explained. "And he does tricks!"

"He followed us and he wants to live here," Flossie added. The white dog jumped from the car and trotted up the walk.

Dinah shook her head dubiously. "I don't know how Mr. Snoop's going to like that!" she said. "You know he's powerful jealous!"

As she spoke the black cat appeared in the doorway of the house. At the sight of the dog, Snoop's back arched, his fur rose, and he stood rigid, barring the way.

"Come on, Snoop!" Bert urged. "The dog's not going to hurt you!"

For reply the cat's back arched even higher.

Bert snapped his fingers. The dog stood on his

hind legs and pranced around. The cat's eyes followed every move. Then the white dog lay down and rolled over in front of Snoop, ending on his back with his paws held helplessly in the air!

Snoop's fur flattened out and he began to purr. The next minute he walked over to the dog and rubbed against his shoulder.

"They're going to be friends!" Freddie cried, running up and throwing his arms around both pets.

Mr. Bobbsey laughed. "It looks as if your new friend has persuaded Snoop that he's harmless!"

The children ran upstairs to get ready for supper while Dinah took the dog out to the kitchen. Soon the two animals were eating side by side.

When Sam came in a little later after delivering his passengers to the railroad station, Mr. Bobbsey said, "Fix the dog a bed in the garage, will you, Sam? We'll keep him here tonight anyway."

At the supper table Flossie spoke up. "What shall we call the doggie? He should have a name so he'll know who he is!"

"Let's call him Bongo!" Freddie suggested.

"Or Shaggy 'cause his fur is!" Flossie said.

"You could call him Wrinkle Nose or Waggle Tail," Mr. Bobbsey said teasingly.

The twins laughed. Then Nan said, "Why not call him Snap because he does tricks when Bert snaps his fingers."

"Yes, and his eyes are snappy," Flossie agreed.

Several other names were suggested but they finally decided that Snap was the best.

"But remember," Mr. Bobbsey cautioned, "the dog isn't yours, and he probably already has a name."

"But Daddy, we can keep him, can't we?" Freddie said in distress. "Snap wants to live with us!"

Mr. Bobbsey shook his head. "That wouldn't be fair, son. The dog seems to be a valuable animal. We'll have to try to find his owner!"

CHAPTER IV

THE NEWSPAPER AD

WHEN Mr. Bobbsey said they should try to find the dog's owner, the twins looked disappointed.

Nan said thoughtfully, "Whoever had Snap must have been very fond of him to teach him so many tricks."

"That's right," Bert agreed. "And he probably feels bad about losing his dog."

Flossie sighed. "I'll feel terrible to lose him, too!"

Mrs. Bobbsey suggested that they wait until morning to do anything about Snap. The children were tired after their exciting day and soon dropped off to sleep.

The next day was bright and sunny. Freddie and Flossie ran out to the garage before breakfast to see Snap. When the small twins opened the door the dog bounded up to them, barking happily. Then he stood on his hind legs and marched a few steps.

"I think he likes it here!" Freddie observed.

Later at the breakfast table the Bobbseys discussed how to find Snap's owner. Remembering Nan's suggestion that the dog might have strayed from the circus train, Bert said, "Maybe we should find out where the circus was going. Then we could write the manager and ask if they have lost a dog."

"But what was the name of the circus and how can we find them?" Nan asked.

"I'll call the railroad station," Bert volunteered. "The stationmaster may know."

He left the table. When he returned a few minutes later, he reported that it had been the Hayden Circus. "When they finally got to Lakeport last night, they loaded the animals in trucks and the performers in buses. The railroad man doesn't know where they went."

"Then I guess we can keep Snap," Freddie said happily.

"Just a minute, my little fireman," Mr. Bobbsey said with a smile. "You'll have to try harder than that to find the dog's owner!"

"We could put an ad in the paper," Bert suggested half-heartedly.

Mr. and Mrs. Bobbsey agreed that this was a

good way to handle it. Nan ran to get paper and pencil, and the twins composed a notice for the "found" column of the newspaper. It read:

FOUND: trick dog. Owner please phone the Bobbsey twins.

After Nan had called the ad in to the paper the twins felt they had done all they could to find out where the shaggy white dog had come from.

School was to open in two days so everyone was very busy. There were clothes to be made ready and summer reports to be finished.

"I'm really glad to go back to school," Bert observed. "It will be fun working for the new museum."

"Yes," said Nan. "And it will be nice to see Nellie and Charlie again."

Nellie Parks, blond and blue-eyed, was Nan's special friend, while dark-haired Charlie Mason was Bert's chum.

On opening day the twins started off early. When they reached the corner near the school they heard a friendly hail. It was from Nellie.

"Hi, Bobbseys!" she called. "Wait for me!"

Nellie had no sooner joined the twins than Charlie came running up. As soon as they had caught up on the summer's news and heard about the trick dog, Nellie said, "I hear you're head of the museum committee, Bert. I'm one of your members!"

"And I'm the other!" Charlie announced with a grin.

"Say, that's great!" Bert declared. "I wonder what we're supposed to do?"

"We'll find out in assembly," Charlie said. "Mr. Tetlow's going to make an announcement about it."

Inside the school Flossie and Freddie ran down the hall to their room while the four older children went to theirs. As they entered, a boy about Bert's age brushed by them. He was Danny Rugg.

Danny was taller and heavier than Bert, and he seemed to enjoy playing mean tricks on the Bobbseys. Now he scowled when Bert spoke to him.

"I suppose you and your sister have been solving mysteries all summer!" he said with a scornful laugh.

Bert kept his temper. "As a matter of fact, we have," he said coolly and walked over to his desk.

Later when the pupils gathered in the auditorium, Mr. Tetlow told them about the new museum and announced the committee. "I hope that many of you will bring in articles for display," he said. "We have some exhibits now, and I shall be glad to show them to you this afternoon."

There was excited conversation about the museum project as the children made their way back to their classrooms.

"I think it's a silly idea," Danny Rugg remarked to his pal Jack Westley. "And Bert Bobbsey's teacher's pet. He's always made head of everything!"

Jack snickered, and Bert, who had overheard the remark, flushed angrily. But he had resolved that he would not let Danny annoy him this year, and so he said nothing.

Nan, however, was worried. "I'm sure Danny will be up to something soon," she thought.

Shortly before the afternoon session began, a white truck stopped in front of the school building. A bell jangled, and a black-haired young man in a sparkling white suit jumped down.

"It's Tony!" Nellie cried. "I was wondering if he'd be back this year!"

Tony was the driver of the ice-cream truck which stopped at the school each noon when the children were returning after lunch at home. He was a great favorite with all of them because he always remembered their names and the ice cream flavors they liked.

"Hi, Tony!" Freddie called, running down to the truck. "I'd like vanilla fudge!"

Soon all the children were gathered around the white truck shouting their orders.

"Just a minute! One at a time!" Tony protested as he opened the back of the truck and reached in for the frozen packages.

"I'd like chocolate mint," Nan decided. "Then Monday I'll have strawberry."

Tony laughed. "That's a good idea. But you'll have to tell the new man on Monday!"

"Oh, Tony, aren't you coming back?" Nellie asked in dismay.

"You can't leave us, Tony!" the other children cried in chorus.

"Oh, I'll be back later," Tony explained. "But next week I'm taking a vacation!"

"Who is the new man?" Nan wanted to know.

Tony explained that he did not know the man but that he had asked to take Tony's place for a week. "He's going to rent another truck. So, with what he's paying me for the route, I'm off for a trip with my family."

At that moment the school bell rang. The children waved good-by to Tony and trooped into the building.

"We'll meet you and Freddie in the museum room after school," Nan told Flossie as she turned into her home room.

An activities room had been newly decorated for the purpose. There were shelves around the sides of the room and several glass cases. When Mr. Tetlow came in, the Bobbseys, Nellie, Charlie, and two little friends of the younger twins, Susie Larker and Teddy Blake, were looking at a vase. It had a large, egg-shaped body and a narrow neck with a handle on each side. A procession of red horses against a background of black encircled the piece.

"I see you like my vase," Mr. Tetlow remarked with a smile. "It's called an amphora and was made in Greece several thousand years ago."

"I like the horses!" Freddie said. "They're chasing each other around the vase."

Mr. Tetlow laughed. "That's right. The scene is a horse race and the amphora was probably given to the winner at the great athletic games which they held in those days."

"I like this statue best," Nan remarked. She picked up a little figure about eight inches tall. It was of a woman with a tiny waist and wide skirt. Her high headdress was a brilliant red while her dress was blue and cream-colored.

"You have good taste, Nan," the principal observed. "That is a statuette of the snake goddess, and it came from the ruins of an ancient palace in Crete."

"Where's Crete?" Freddie asked.

Mr. Tetlow explained that Crete was an island in the Mediterranean Sea near Greece. "This statuette is the most valuable thing in the museum. A friend of mine, Mr. Thomas Nelson, has loaned it to us while he is in Europe."

As the Bobbsey twins continued their tour of the room, Bert admired a collection of Indian flints and arrowheads. Freddie and Teddy pressed their noses against a glass case to get a better look at some bows and arrows. Charlie examined a group of early American coins.

Finally when they had looked at everything in the room, the children thanked Mr. Tetlow and started home. "Why don't you all stop at our house and play awhile?" Nan suggested to the twins' friends.

"Yes," Flossie said mischievously, "I saw Dinah baking some cookies this morning."

The eight children walked into the Bobbseys' back yard. Dinah came to the kitchen door with a broad smile on her face.

"Looks like I got some customers for my fresh cookies!" she remarked. "You all sit down around the picnic table, and I'll bring you a little snack."

Nan ran in to help, and in a few minutes she and Dinah came out carrying a plate of cookies, a tray of glasses, and a big pitcher of milk.

"Boy! That looks good!" Charlie exclaimed as they settled around the table.

Talk about the new museum went on as the

children drank the milk and munched the cookies.

"We'll have to get busy and find some more things for it," Bert said as he finished eating.

"Yes, the room does look sort of empty," Charlie agreed.

"We can ask everyone at school to bring in exhibits," Nellie proposed enthusiastically.

"It would be nice to have some things which would belong to the school and stay in the museum permanently," Nan spoke up.

"But where will we get the money to buy anything?" Charlie objected.

"We ought to be able to think of some way to raise money!" Nan insisted.

Nellie looked thoughtful for a moment. "I have an idea!"

CHAPTER V

THE MISSING STATUE

THE children turned toward Nellie. "We might have a white elephant sale," she proposed.

"But where would we find a white elephant, and who would buy him?" Flossie asked.

The older children laughed at the idea of a real white elephant, but Freddie spoke up in defense of his twin. "What's so funny about that?" he asked.

Nan explained that a white elephant sale was one to which people brought things they did not want. Then other people who might like the articles bought them.

"But where is the elephant?" Flossie persisted, still puzzled.

"There isn't a real elephant, honey," Nan said. "It's an old saying that things people have no further use for are no more good to them than a white elephant would be."

Freddie chuckled. "Then Danny Rugg's a white elephant of ours!"

The others laughed, and Bert suggested with a grin, "Maybe we can sell Danny!"

"Nobody'd want him!" Charlie said scornfully.

"We might have a cookie sale," Flossie proposed.

"We've had those before," Nan objected. "Let's do something different!"

There was silence for a few minutes while the children thought about ways to earn money. Charlie finally spoke up, "How about a circus?"

"That's good," Bert replied, "except that it might be too much work."

"A circus would be fun, though," Nan mused. Then she sat up straight as an idea came to her. "I know!" she cried. "We can have a puppet show. I saw directions for making puppets in a magazine Mother had."

"That would be exciting!" Nellie declared.

Nan began to describe how puppets are constructed. The others listened intently. Suddenly Nellie looked up and laughed.

"Is this your trick dog?" she asked.

Snap, holding a stick in his mouth, was hopping across the lawn on his hind legs. When he reached Nan, he dropped the stick and looked up expectantly. Nan picked it up and threw his stick as far as she could. With a scurry, Snap ran after the stick, grabbed it, and returned to Nan.

"Let's see his other tricks!" Charlie urged.

Bert snapped his fingers. Immediately Snap rose to his hind legs and marched in a circle. Then when the twins clapped their hands, the dog dropped to the ground and rolled over. Next he sat down in front of Bert and held out his paw to shake hands.

"He's the best dog I ever saw!" Susie cried.

"Maybe he'd jump through a hoop," Nellie suggested.

"We'll try it!" said Bert. He ran into the house and returned shortly with a red hoop of Flossie's. Snap gave an excited bark.

"Come on, boy!" Bert called, snapping his fingers and holding out the hoop.

The dog ran a little way down the yard. Then he turned around and raced toward Bert. When he got there he rose gracefully into the air and sailed through the hoop.

"Say, he's really sharp!" Charlie commented admiringly, and they all applauded.

"We think maybe he's been in a circus," Nan explained.

Evidently feeling that he had done enough tricks, Snap walked to the end of the yard and lay down under a bush. Snoop, who had been watching from a branch of the apple tree, jumped to the ground. He walked over to Snap and settled himself comfortably at the dog's side.

Flossie had an idea. "Why don't Freddie and Susie and Teddy and I run a pet show? Freddie, you and I can make Snap do some tricks. The

other children in school can bring their special
pets and we can have prizes for the best!"

"I'll bring my turtle," Teddy Blake offered.

"I'll bring Fluffy, my kitty," Susie decided.

"I know something else we can do!" Flossie's
blue eyes sparkled with mischief.

"What?"

Flossie motioned the younger children over
to the side of the yard and whispered. Susie and
Teddy giggled. Then Freddie said, "That's a
good idea, Floss. We'll do it!"

"What are you four going to do?" Nan asked
when she heard him.

"We're—"

"No, don't tell, Freddie!" Flossie protested.
"It's a secret!"

At this moment Dinah came to the back door.
"Susie," she called, "your mother wants you to
come home. She just telephoned."

"I guess we'd all better go," Nellie said. "I'm
glad we decided to have the shows. It will be
fun."

"Okay, we'll make the puppets next week,"
Nan said as she walked to the front of the
house with her friend.

Charlie and Nellie turned one way while
Susie and Teddy walked in the other direction.
"See you Monday, Flossie!" Susie called.

Nan walked over to Bert and said in a low voice, "I hope we won't hear anything from the newspaper ad. It would be a shame if Snap's taken away before our show."

"Right," said Bert.

But no call or letter came from the dog's owner over the week end.

Early Monday morning Dinah called Bert to the phone. "It's Mrs. Mason," she told him.

Charlie's mother said that her son twisted his ankle the evening before. "I think he should stay off it today. He wants you to bring him the paper bag he left in his desk."

"Yes, Mrs. Mason," Bert replied. "I'll bring it at noon. I'm sorry about Charlie's ankle."

But at noon Bert hurried home with the other twins and forgot Charlie's message. On the way back to school after lunch he suddenly remembered. "I'll get it now," he said to Nan. "There's still time to run over to the Masons'."

"Okay," said Nan. "There's the ice-cream truck. I'll go over there."

Bert ran into the school building and Nan wandered over to a white panel truck where a group of children had gathered.

The driver already had opened the back and was selling the ice-cream sticks from a freezer in the truck. He had rather dirty-looking blond hair, and his white coveralls were not too clean.

"I'll be glad when Tony comes back," Nan said to Nellie as the two girls stood eating their ice cream. "This man doesn't seem very nice!"

Suddenly the man turned to Danny Rugg, who was standing nearby. "Will you sell these things for me, sonny?" he asked. "I just remembered my wife wants me to pick up some frozen food at that grocery on the other side of the school. Just take in the money. I'll be back in a few minutes."

Danny beamed. "Sure," he said. "I'll be glad to."

After the man had left, Danny motioned to Jack Westley and several other special pals. "Step up, fellows," he called, "and have some free ice cream!"

"You're not supposed to give that ice cream away, Danny!" Nellie protested.

"Mind your own business!" Danny said rudely. "*I'm* the one he asked to help him!"

"Sure, Danny, I'll have chocolate!" Jack Westley called with a smirk.

In a few minutes Danny was doing a brisk business with his pals. The other children looked on, alarmed. Finally Nan and Nellie walked away in disgust.

Bert came out of the building with Charlie's package under his arm. He stopped to speak to the girls just as Freddie and Flossie, followed by Snap, came up.

"I'd like some ice cream," Freddie said wistfully, "but I forgot to bring my money!"

"I'll buy you some," Bert offered. "I'll treat you and Flossie and you can pay me back when we get home," he added with a grin.

"But that's not treating!" Flossie objected.

"Bert's teasing you," Nan said. "I'm sure he'll buy you some ice cream. But wait until the man comes back. Don't get mixed up with Danny!"

Bert caught sight of Snap, who was running around among the children. "You shouldn't have brought Snap. He can't go to school!"

Flossie giggled. "He's smart enough!"

"He followed us," Freddie explained, "and we couldn't make him go back!"

"Oh well, he'll probably leave when we go into the building," Bert said as he started off toward Charlie's house.

Just then the blond truck driver came hurrying up. He was carrying a paper parcel. Quickly he put it into the back of the truck and slammed the door. Then he looked around for Danny.

"Where's the kid who was selling for me?" he asked curtly.

Danny came forward and sheepishly put a few coins in the man's hand. The driver stuck them into his pocket without counting and hurriedly climbed up onto the truck seat.

Danny shot Nellie a look of triumph. He had gotten away with his little trick!

At that moment Snap came trotting up. "Woof! Woof!" he barked fiercely and ran toward the truck.

The ice-cream man paid no attention to the dog and started the engine. Snap gave a flying leap and landed on the seat beside the man. Bert, attracted by the noise, looked back.

"Get out of here!" the driver snarled at Snap. He gave the dog a violent shove which sent him sprawling to the ground. Then the man started the truck and headed for the dog.

"Snap!" Nan screamed. "Get out of the way!"

Snap gathered himself together and managed to scramble out of the way of the oncoming truck. It sped down the street.

In a flash Bert pulled a small notebook from his pocket and wrote down the license number of the truck.

"That was the meanest thing I ever saw!" he

said hotly. "I ought to report him to the police!"

"Thank goodness Snap wasn't hurt!" Nan said, leaning down and hugging the dog.

"Why did Snap bark at that man?" Flossie asked.

Bert shrugged. "I don't know. Maybe the man reminded Snap of someone he doesn't like! See you later. I'll have to run all the way to Charlie's to get back before the bell rings!"

Bert made good time and slipped into his home room just as the teacher, Miss Vandermeer, was closing the door.

When classes were over for the day Nan said to her twin, "Nellie and I are going to the store to buy the material for our puppets. I'll see you at home."

Bert packed his books and homework assignments, then turned toward the museum room.

"Everyone's gone home. I guess I can lock up now," he decided.

When Bert reached the room he gave a quick glance around before turning out the lights. Everything seemed to be in order. Then suddenly he noticed something was wrong.

The valuable statue of the Cretan snake goddess was missing!

CHAPTER VI

SNAP DRESSES UP

"BUT the statue can't be gone!" Bert thought in dismay. "Who would take it?" He searched frantically around the room, but there was no sign of the little figure.

Bert ran down the hall to the principal's office. The secretary had left, but the door to Mr. Tetlow's private office was open. Bert dashed in.

Mr. Tetlow looked up from some papers he was reading. "What's the matter, Bert?" he asked. "You seem upset!"

Bert blurted out his story of the missing statuette. Mr. Tetlow jumped to his feet. "That figure gone!" he exclaimed. "That's the most valuable thing we have in the museum! We must find it!"

The principal hurried from his office, followed by Bert. Mr. Tetlow looked carefully on each shelf in the museum room and opened all the cupboards. The statuette was not there!

"We'll search the whole building," he decided. "Perhaps this is someone's idea of a joke!"

Together he and Bert looked into every classroom and storage place, but they did not find the missing snake goddess. Finally Mr. Tetlow summoned the janitor.

"Mr. Carter," the principal said to the short, jolly-looking man, "have any strangers been in the building today?"

The man stared up at the ceiling as he thought. Then he said, "Yes, there were two. A man was here trying to sell me a new kind of floor wax. And there was an inspector from the electric light company."

"Did either of them go into the museum?" Bert asked eagerly.

The janitor reported that he had taken the salesman in to look at the floors and that the man from the electric company had said he was going all over the building to check the lights.

"What did these men look like?" Mr. Tetlow asked.

"Well, let me see." Mr. Carter pondered a moment. "The floor-wax man was about my height and had light hair. The other man was bald. He wore blue coveralls."

"Do you think one of them took the statuette?" Bert asked anxiously, looking at Mr. Tetlow.

"It's hard to tell."

"Why don't we call the companies and find out about the men?" Bert suggested eagerly.

"That's a good idea," Mr. Tetlow declared. "I remember you're pretty good at solving mysteries, Bert. Maybe you can solve this one!"

Mr. Carter told Bert the wax company's number, and he called it. The head of the sales department said that he had sent the salesman to the school that day and that he was a very reliable man.

Bert thanked him, then called the electric company. When he asked about the man who had come to check the lights, the official said, "I don't know what you mean. We haven't sent anyone out to check lights!"

"You don't have an inspector who's bald and wears blue coveralls?" Bert persisted.

"No one like that in our employ!" the light company man insisted.

Bert put down the phone and cried out, "It must have been that phony electric company man! How can we find him?"

"The first thing to do is notify the police," Mr. Tetlow stated firmly.

When Chief Mahoney came on the line, the

principal reported the theft of the valuable figure. The officer said he would send a man up at once.

"You'd better stay awhile, Bert," Mr. Tetlow advised. "You may be able to help."

In a short time a police car stopped in front of the school, and an officer hurried into the building. He introduced himself as Jim Murphy.

"Just where was this statue when it was stolen?" he asked briskly.

Mr. Tetlow and Bert led the way to the museum and showed him the shelf where the snake goddess had been displayed. Officer Murphy looked around the room.

"I'm afraid it's impossible to tell anything from fingerprints. There are too many." He looked puzzled. "You say this is the only thing missing?"

Bert nodded.

"It is also the article worth the most money," Mr. Tetlow added. "It seems as though whoever stole the statue knew its value."

In reply to further questioning by Officer Murphy, Bert told about the mysterious man who had come to check the lights. "The electric company says they didn't send anyone," he added.

After getting a description from the janitor of the man in the blue coveralls, Officer Murphy closed his little notebook. "We'll send out an alarm for a man answering that description," he said. "We should be able to pick him up soon."

While all this was going on at school, Freddie and Flossie were at home. "What shall we play now?" Freddie asked his twin as they wandered onto the back porch of the Bobbseys' big house.

"We could play house. I'll be the mother, and Snap and Snoop can be our children!"

"I don't want to do that," Freddie said glumly. "A dog and cat would be silly children!"

At this moment Flossie noticed a bundle of clothes in a corner of the porch. "What are these for?" she called to Dinah, who was busy in the kitchen.

"Your mother left them there. Someone was supposed to pick them up for a rummage sale," was the reply.

An impish look came into Flossie's blue eyes. "Let's dress up Snap!" she suggested. "I see my old blue party dress. I think Snap would look pretty in it!"

"Say, that would be fun!" Freddie exclaimed. "A dog dressed up. Let's do it!"

While Flossie pulled the dress from the bundle, Freddie ran to the end of the yard where Snap was asleep. At Freddie's urging, the dog got up and followed the little boy back to the porch.

Freddie held him as Flossie slipped the fluffy blue dress over his head and pushed his front paws through the little sleeves. Then she fastened the dress down the dog's back.

Snap, entering into the game, stood on his hind legs and waved his front paws in the air.

Flossie giggled. "Doesn't he look funny?" She turned to the bundle of clothes again and picked up a white straw bonnet with little blue flowers around the crown. "I think he needs a hat!"

She placed the bonnet on Snap's shaggy white head and tied the blue ribbon streamers under his jaw.

Freddie grabbed a white cloth handbag from the bundle and held it in front of Snap. The dog leaned forward and took it between his teeth.

"Look at him!" Freddie and Flossie doubled over with laughter.

Snap, evidently proud of his costume, took off down the driveway, hopping along on his hind legs, the white purse swinging from his mouth.

A boy, riding past the house on his bicycle, turned to look at the strange sight. He lost control of the bike, and almost skidded into a woman stepping from the sidewalk. He fell flat.

Caught by surprise the woman dropped a bag of groceries she was carrying. Oranges and apples rolled down the street.

"Oh! Oh!" she cried, trying to keep from tripping over the fallen bicycle.

Upset by the commotion, Snap dropped to all fours and dashed around the corner of the house. Freddie and Flossie ran down to the street and picked up the fruit. The boy with the bicycle had scrambled to his feet and pulled his machine upright.

"We're awf'ly sorry our dog made everything happen," Flossie said, as she put the oranges back into the bag.

"That's all right," the woman said with a twinkle in her eye. "I can't blame the boy for falling off his bike. It isn't often one sees a dog like that one!"

"Snap's a trick dog!" Freddie explained proudly.

When he and his twin reached the back yard again Dinah was standing in the kitchen doorway, her hands on her hips. "You children take those good clothes right off that dog!" she ordered sternly. "And fix up that bundle again."

Then she softened. "If you want something to do, you can sprinkle the front lawn. It's getting mighty brown!"

Quickly the children undressed Snap, and Dinah said she would launder the dress before putting it back into the bundle. Freddie and

Flossie ran around to the front yard. Snap trotted after them.

Freddie attached the hose to the outlet and began to water the flower borders. Flossie picked up a long stick. Snap watched her eagerly, making little whining sounds.

"I wonder if he wants to jump over it?" Flossie called out to her twin.

"Try him!" Freddie urged.

Flossie held the stick straight out about two feet off the ground. Snap backed away, then ran forward and leaped over the stick.

"Snap has another trick!" Flossie cried.

"Maybe he'll jump over the water from the hose!" Freddie suggested. "I'll squirt it out straight. You stand on the other side and call Snap."

Flossie did this but Snap did not seem to want to jump over the water. He hopped about, barking sharply. But he would not do the trick.

"Come on, Snappy!" Flossie urged. "You won't get wet if you jump high enough!"

Freddie lowered the stream and Flossie called again. This time the dog leaped over the stream of water. Then he turned around and leaped back again.

"See! He likes it!" Flossie cried, clapping her hands.

Snap continued to jump back and forth until he was dripping wet. Dinah came to the front door to see what was going on. As Flossie ran toward her, Snap followed. He caught up with the little girl and shook himself vigorously.

"Oh!" Flossie exclaimed. "Stop! You're getting me all wet!"

Freddie, forgetting he still held the hose, turned in Flossie's direction. She jumped aside to escape the water and slipped on the wet grass.

"Land sakes!" Dinah declared. "Flossie, you come in the house this minute and get on some dry clothes!"

After Flossie left, Freddie returned to sprinkling the flower beds and the lawn. He had nearly finished when Danny Rugg came along. He stopped in front of the Bobbseys' house.

"Hi, Freddie!" Danny said cheerfully.

Freddie, who did not trust Danny, muttered a greeting and went on with his work.

"Jack Westley just told me that Greek figure in the museum has been stolen! He was still at school and heard all the excitement," Danny volunteered.

Freddie said nothing.

"And I know who stole it, too!" Danny said.

"Who?" Freddie asked curiously.

"Your brother Bert!"

CHAPTER VII

PING-PONG PUPPETS

"MY brother never stole anything!" Freddie declared hotly.

"Oh, no?" Danny replied with a sneer. "Well, I saw him with my own eyes coming out of school at noon with a package under his arm. And it *wasn't* his lunch!"

"He was taking something to Charlie Mason!" Freddie's voice rose to a shout.

"A likely story!" Danny jeered.

By this time Freddie was so furious he could hardly speak. He wanted to fight Danny but knew he was too little. There was something else he could do, though! Quick as a wink he turned the hose directly on Danny!

"You get out of here!" he cried.

Danny, caught by surprise, stood still for a second in the spray from the hose. Then with a yell he jumped aside. His clothes were soaked, and water dripped from his face.

"I'll get even with you for this, Freddie Bobbsey!" Danny yelled. He shook his fist and ran off down the street.

Snap, who had been watching the two boys eagerly, bounded after Danny, barking fiercely.

"Come back, Snap!" Freddie called. Reluctantly the dog returned.

Nan was late getting home from her shopping trip with Nellie. It was suppertime when Bert arrived, so the twins had no chance to talk before going to the table.

"What's the matter, son?" Mr. Bobbsey asked. "You look very glum!"

Bert explained about the disappearance of the ancient statuette from Crete. "And I'm supposed to be in charge of the museum!" he ended gloomily.

"That was my favorite exhibit!" Nan commented sadly.

"Danny says you took it, Bert," Freddie spoke up. "But I turned the hose on him for saying it, and he ran!"

"Freddie!" Mrs. Bobbsey exclaimed. "What do you mean?"

When Freddie told of his meeting with Danny that afternoon and how it had ended, Flossie giggled. "Danny must have been s'prised when he got all wet!"

"That was a very naughty thing to do, Freddie!" Mrs. Bobbsey said sternly. "You know Danny likes to tease. You should pay no attention to him!"

Bert and Nan had a different opinion. They were sure Danny would spread the story about Bert. But they said nothing.

"Who do you suppose did take the figure?" Mr. Bobbsey wondered. "Could it be a joke?"

Bert shook his head. "I don't think so. Mr. Tetlow and I looked all over the building before we called the police. We all think it was the man who pretended to be from the electric company."

Conversation turned to other topics, and nothing more was said about the missing statuette. But Bert did not forget what Freddie had said.

At noon the next day as he was leaving the school building, he challenged Danny. "I hear you think I stole the statue!" Bert said angrily.

"Yes, I do, and I'm going to tell the police!" the bully declared. "Your little brother can't turn the hose on me and get away with it!"

"You'd better apologize for what you said about me!" Bert persisted.

"Who's going to make me?"

By this time the boys had reached the play

yard. Danny gave Bert a shove which sent him staggering against the side of the building.

Bert regained his balance and advanced on Danny with clenched fists. He punched the bully on the arm. Although Bert was smaller than Danny, he was strong. Stung by the blow, Danny lashed out violently.

"What's going on here?" a stern voice asked. Both boys turned quickly. Mr. Tetlow walked toward them.

"He started it!" Danny said with a whine.

Mr. Tetlow looked at Bert. "What's the meaning of this?" he asked.

Bert told the principal of Danny's accusation.

"I'm ashamed of you, Danny," Mr. Tetlow said. "You know Bert didn't take that statue! Now apologize to him and go on home to lunch!"

Danny muttered something and hurried away.

Mr. Tetlow put his hand on Bert's shoulder. "Don't worry about the statuette," he said kindly. "I'm sure the police will find it."

At the end of the afternoon session Nan called to Bert and Charlie as they were leaving their classroom. "Nellie and I got some things for making puppets. Do you fellows want to help us?" she asked.

The boys agreed, and soon the four children were settled around the Bobbseys' dining room table. Paste, crayons, and bits of material were strewn about.

"What are the Ping-pong balls for?" Charlie asked in surprise.

"They're what we use to make the heads," Nellie explained. "The man at the store made holes in them so one of our fingers will fit in. We draw faces on the balls, fasten a costume to each one, then work them with our hands."

After some discussion the children decided to make four puppets—one for each of them to manage. Bert said he would make a clown puppet, and Charlie chose a policeman. Nan and Nellie thought they would make animals— Nan an ostrich and Nellie a kitten.

Bert's was the easiest to do. He drew a wide red mouth on the Ping-pong ball, a round black mark for a nose, and big, staring eyes. Then he folded a bit of red paper into the shape of a clown's hat and pasted it onto the head.

"I'll make the suit if you'll fix the ostrich head," Nan offered.

Bert grinned and set to work. First he covered the ball with gray crayon and drew large eyes with long lashes on them. Then he made a wide bill from a piece of brown paper and pasted it on.

"This will be the long neck," he said, holding up a cardboard tube. He fastened one end of this to the hole in the Ping-pong ball.

By this time Nan had finished the clown suit. It was made of red-and-white dotted cloth, and at the ends of the arms she fastened tiny hands of red cloth stuffed with cotton.

Bert pasted the suit to the head. Then he stuck his index finger into the hole at the back. He put his middle finger and thumb into the two arms.

"Ho! Ho!" he laughed, making the clown's hands beat against its chest while the head tossed back and forth.

"That's great, Bert!" Charlie said admiringly. "But wait until I finish my policeman! Then your clown won't be laughing!"

Charlie had colored his Ping-pong ball tan. Now he drew a red button nose, black dots for eyes, and a red line for a mouth. Next he ravelled a bit of cord and pasted it over the mouth for a mustache. A piece of blue paper formed a cap.

"He's wonderful!" Nellie cried when Charlie held up his policeman's head. "Can you make a kitten's head for me?"

While Charlie worked on this, the two girls sewed the bodies for the other three puppets.

Suddenly Nellie looked at the clock. "Oh!" she exclaimed. "It's getting late. I'd better go home."

Charlie decided he should leave also. Bert and Nan walked to the door with them, then went back to the dining room to straighten up.

"It's been almost a week since we put that ad about Snap in the paper," Nan observed, "and we haven't had any reply."

"I hope that means he doesn't belong to anyone and we can keep him!" Bert said as he put the top on the paste jar.

All this time Freddie and Flossie had been at Susie Larker's house to play. Now they came running up the walk to the front door. As Freddie turned the knob, Flossie leaned over to pick something up from the porch floor.

"It's a letter!" she said. "It must have dropped out of the mailbox!"

The small twins ran into the dining room with it. "Here's a letter," Flossie said. "Ooh lookee! It says for the Bobbsey twins!" She handed it to Nan.

"Open the letter and read it, sis!" Bert urged.

With a puzzled expression Nan tore open the envelope and pulled out a piece of lined tablet paper. She quickly read the few lines of writing.

"Oh dear!" she cried. "It's from a man who says he thinks we have his trick dog!"

"Who is he?" Bert asked.

"Where does he live?" Freddie wanted to know.

"You mean Snap belongs to him?" Flossie cried, her eyes beginning to fill with tears.

Nan studied the sheet of paper again, then turned the envelope over in her hand. "That's funny," she said finally. "He doesn't give any address or telephone number."

"What's his name?" Bert asked.

"James Smith."

"Maybe we can find him in the phone book."

Bert went to the hall table to get it. He flipped the pages until he came to the Smiths. He ran his finger down the column.

"There are five James Smiths," he announced.

"I suppose we'll have to call them all," Nan observed sadly.

"I want to call first!" Flossie declared. "May I, Nan?"

When Nan nodded, Flossie ran to the hall phone and dialed the numbers as Bert called them out. There was a long wait, then a little voice said, "Hello."

"Is this James Smith?" Flossie asked. "And did you lose a dog?"

"I'm Sally Smith," the voice replied. "I don't have a dog!"

"Sally!" Flossie exclaimed. "This is Flossie!" Sally and Flossie were in the same room at school. "Are you sure your daddy didn't write us a letter about Snap?"

"I don't think so," came the uncertain reply, "but I'll ask him when he comes home."

"You have the wrong Smith, Flossie!" Nan whispered. "Say good-by and hang up!"

When Flossie had done so, Freddie took his

turn. The James Smith he called had a quavery voice. "What's that you say?" he asked.

Freddie repeated the question. "Haven't had a dog since I was a little shaver," came the reply. "I'm getting old now, but if you want to get rid o' your dog, I'll take him!" The man gave a cackling laugh.

"Oh, no!" Freddie cried. "We want to *keep* him!" The little boy put down the phone.

Bert made the next call, and a woman answered. When Bert asked for James Smith, she said, "James Smith hasn't been here for six months. What do you want him for?"

The boy explained about the letter which they had received. "I don't know anything about any dog," the woman said sharply, "and I don't want to be bothered about James Smith!" With that she slammed the receiver.

"Well, we're not having much luck!" Bert remarked as he and Nan made the last two calls.

"No one seems to be missing a trick dog."

"You know something?" Nan said thoughtfully. "I don't think any James Smith *wrote* that letter!"

CHAPTER VIII

BERT'S CLEVER TRAP

"WHAT makes you think James Smith didn't write the letter, Nan?" Bert asked curiously.

"Because the writing just doesn't look like a man's. And if the person *really* thought Snap was his dog, he would have given us his address!" Nan said convincingly.

Bert took the letter and examined it carefully. "I think maybe you're right," he said finally. "And I'll bet I know who sent it."

"Danny Rugg!"

Bert nodded grimly.

"Then we still can keep Snap!" Flossie cried.

"Yes, if we can think of some way to *prove* the letter is a trick," Bert mused. He thought for a minute, then his face lighted up. "I have an idea how I can find out for sure!"

He told the other twins his plan. Nan laughed. "That should trap Danny if he really *is* the one who wrote the note!"

69

The next morning on the way to school Bert told Nellie and Charlie what he was going to do. Then before the bell rang he had a conversation with Miss Vandermeer.

When the children were assembled in the room, the teacher told them that Bert had an announcement to make. He stood up.

"You know Mr. Tetlow said he hoped all of us could bring something to exhibit in the museum," he began. "Nellie, Charlie, and I would like to know what you have. So will each of you write down anything you can contribute?"

There was much scurrying for paper and pencils, and the scribbling began. When all had finished, Charlie collected the papers and gave them to Bert.

"Thank you," Bert said. "The committee will look at them and let you know what we think we can use."

At recess time Nan joined the three committee members in a corner of the room where they were sorting out the pieces of paper. There were all sorts of suggestions.

"Say!" Charlie exclaimed. "Ned Brown has a rattlesnake skin! That would be great!"

"And one of the girls has an embroidered shawl from Spain!" Nellie held up one of the notes.

"But where is Danny's paper?" Nan asked.

"Here it is!" Nellie exclaimed, holding up a piece of lined tablet paper. A large NOTH-ING was scrawled across it!

Nan took the paper while Bert pulled the mysterious letter from his pocket. They laid them on a desk side by side. The paper and the writing matched perfectly!

"So it *was* Danny!" Nan said.

"You Bobbseys should do something to teach Danny a lesson!" Nellie remarked. "He's always getting away with mean tricks like this!"

"Yes," Charlie agreed. "We'll help you get even with him. Let's think of something!"

But before anyone could make a suggestion, the bell signaling the end of the recess period rang. The other children came in and took their seats. Danny was the last to arrive, and he looked flustered.

"Something's happened!" Nan whispered to Bert. Her twin shrugged and slipped into his seat.

During recess Freddie and Flossie had met the bully in the hall.

"Hi!" Danny had hailed them in a friendly fashion. "How's the little hose squirter?" he said to Freddie. "That was a good trick you played on me yesterday!"

Freddie looked a little shamefaced but said nothing.

"I'll show you another good trick," Danny offered.

"What is it?" Freddie asked uncertainly. He was suspicious of Danny but also curious about the trick.

Danny led the small twins to a drinking fountain which stood against the wall of the corridor.

"See this?" he asked, pointing to the spout where the water came out.

Freddie nodded.

"Well, you step on the pedal to start the water," Danny explained, "while you put your finger over the hole. Go on! Do it and see what happens!"

Freddie looked doubtful, but he put his finger over the spout and stepped on the pedal. The water spurted in all directions!

Mr. Tetlow had just come from his office and started down the hall. A long stream of cold water caught him in the eye! With a gasp Danny fled down the hall and disappeared into his home room.

"Freddie Bobbsey!" Mr. Tetlow said in a stern voice. "Come into my office!"

Followed by Flossie, Freddie walked slowly into the principal's office. Mr. Tetlow sat down behind his desk and looked sternly at the little boy.

"Don't you know that it is against the rules of this school to play with the water fountain?"

Freddie hung his head. "Y-y-yes," he confessed, "but I didn't know it was going to act like that!"

Flossie spoke up. "It wasn't Freddie's fault, Mr. Tetlow! Danny Rugg said he'd show him a good trick. Freddie didn't know what it was."

Mr. Tetlow sighed. "Danny Rugg again!

Why is he always getting you Bobbseys into trouble?"

"Because he's a meanie!" Flossie declared.

"Then stay away from him," Mr. Tetlow advised. "All right, Freddie," he continued, "I'll let it go this time. But if I ever see you playing with that drinking fountain again, you will be punished!"

Freddie gulped. "Yes, sir," he said. "I promise never to do it again."

"All right. You and Flossie go back to your room. I'll see Danny Rugg later."

The small twins ran down the hall and managed to slip into their room just before the teacher closed the door. On the way home for lunch Flossie told Bert about Danny's trick.

"We're going to have to do something about Mr. Danny Rugg!" Bert declared. "But you and Freddie stay as far away from him as you can!"

Flossie promised to do this. Freddie was silent.

After lunch Bert met Mr. Tetlow in the hall. "Have you heard anything about the statue?" the boy asked seriously.

"Not a word," the principal replied.

"May I call the police?" Bert asked. "Maybe they've found something and haven't told us."

"Go ahead," Mr. Tetlow agreed. "In fact, come into my office and do it now!"

Bert put in the call and in a few minutes was connected with Chief Mahoney. He asked what progress had been made in finding the thief who had taken the little goddess statue. The officer told him that they had found no clue.

"But we had a report from the police over in Sanderville that they've had thefts from the museum there too," the man continued. "Sounds as if the same man did both jobs."

"Why do you think that?" Bert asked.

"Well, in both cases only the most valuable exhibits have been taken," the chief said. "The thief is evidently a man who knows something about art."

Bert thanked the chief and hung up. When he told Mr. Tetlow the details of the conversation, the principal sighed. "I hope they catch the thief before Mr. Nelson comes back from Europe. I wouldn't like to have to tell him his snake goddess is gone!"

Bert got back to his home room just before the bell rang. Danny was bragging about being a great ball player.

With a wink at Bert, Charlie Mason spoke up, "Okay, Danny, how about all the kids in this room having a game at recess?"

Everyone agreed to this, and when the bell rang for the play period, sides were hurriedly chosen. Danny and Bert were on one team with Nellie, while Nan and Charlie were picked for the opposing team.

The time was almost up, and the sides were even when Nan came to bat. Bert was the pitcher.

"At'ta girl!" Charlie yelled. "Here's your chance to win the game!"

On Bert's first pitch Nan pulled back the bat, then swung with all her might. *Wham!* The bat hit the ball with a crack and Nan rounded the bases. A home run!

"Still think you're so good, Danny?" Charlie asked teasingly as they went into the school building. "A girl won the game!"

Danny scowled and slid into his seat.

When classes were over, the older Bobbseys, Charlie, and Nellie met in a room assigned to them to use for putting together their show. Bert and Nan had brought the puppets to school so they might rehearse with their two friends.

Freddie and Flossie stood outside the building until all the children had left. "Bert's awful upset about the man's stealing that statue!" Flossie said sadly. "I wish we could help him."

"Maybe we can!" Freddie observed. "We know how to look for clues!"

"All right," Flossie agreed. "Let's do it!"

The two children went back into the school and down the hall to the museum room. "We need a magnifying glass!" Freddie said importantly. "Detectives always have those when they look for clues!"

"Daddy has one," Flossie reminded her twin. "Maybe he'll let us bring it to school tomorrow."

Freddie and Flossie walked slowly around the room, peering at all the shelves and examining the floor.

"Here's a hankie!" Flossie called out, picking up a small white square. "And there's a name on it!"

"I'll bet the thief dropped it!" Freddie said excitedly. "What's the name?"

Flossie looked at the handkerchief in her hand and began to giggle. "It says Flossie! It's mine!"

Freddie looked disgusted. "That's no clue!" he protested. Then he stooped to pick up a bit of paper which lay behind the door at the edge of the floor. It was a chewing gum wrapper.

"Here's something! I'll bet the thief dropped this!"

His twin ran to look. "Oh, Freddie! Anyone could have dropped that! It's only a gum wrapper!"

"But we're not allowed to have gum in school," Freddie reminded her. "And, anyway, I never saw any of our friends chewing this kind. Let's see if we can find anything else."

The twins walked into all the classrooms and the auditorium. They found school books, notebooks, old gloves and scarves, and all sorts of misplaced articles, but nothing else which looked as if it might have been dropped by the thief.

"We should look outside under the museum window," Freddie suggested finally. "The thief might have left some footprints."

The children ran out of the building and around to the side. The ground under the window showed no sign of footprints, and the planting around it was undisturbed.

"I guess he didn't go in the window," Flossie remarked.

They started toward the rear door. As they reached it Flossie's eyes were caught by something in the shrubbery. She reached into the prickly bushes and picked it up.

"What's this?" she said in bewilderment.

CHAPTER IX

FLOSSIE'S DISCOVERY

FLOSSIE picked up a torn piece of flesh-colored rubber. Around the edge was what appeared to be human hair.

"Ugh!" the little girl cried as she held the strange find at arm's length. "What is it?"

Freddie took it from her. "Maybe you've found a clue!" he said excitedly. "Let's see what Bert thinks it is!"

The small twins dashed into the school building and along the hall until they came to the room where Bert and Nan were rehearsing.

"Look what Flossie found!" Freddie cried, bursting through the doorway.

Nan put down the ostrich puppet. "You're a regular cyclone! What's the matter?"

Quieting down a little, Freddie explained that he and Flossie had been hunting for clues to the thief who took the snake goddess. "And

Flossie saw this in the shrubbery by the back door!" he ended.

Bert took the object from his brother and turned it over in his hands. "I think it's from a wig," he said.

"But it has only a little hair," Nan objected as the younger children gathered around Bert.

"It's a bald wig!" he explained. "You know, one a man would wear to make himself look bald."

"Bert!" Nan cried. "Didn't Mr. Carter say that the phony electrician who was here the day the statue was stolen was bald?"

"Why, yes." Bert's eyes gleamed. "You mean he might have been wearing a wig and this is part of it?"

Nan nodded excitedly. "If the man wasn't really bald, he could even have been that ice-cream man!"

"The ice-cream man!" Nellie repeated.

"That's right! The statue was taken the day he was here! And I remember when he came back to the truck he was carrying a package! And he hasn't been back since!"

"But he said he was going to the grocery on the next block to buy some food for his wife," Nellie reminded her.

"And Mr. Carter said the electrician's coveralls were blue while the ice-cream man's were white," Bert added. "So how could he have been the same man?"

"We could check at the grocery and see if he did go there," Nan suggested.

Freddie and Flossie had been listening wide-eyed. Now they ran to the door.

"Come on!" Freddie called. "Let's go to the store!"

"No use in all of us going," said Nan. "Why don't Flossie and I talk to the grocer?"

"Okay," the others agreed.

Nan and Flossie walked down the street to the grocery. It was a fairly small one which had recently been made into a self-service market. When Nan and Flossie entered, the place was empty except for the cashier, who seemed to be very busy adding a column of figures. She did not look up.

"I wonder where the manager is?" Flossie whispered.

"He'll probably be here in a few minutes," Nan replied. "We'll have to wait."

The store was divided into two parts by a long partition of shelves. These were filled with cans and bottles of food. At the far end of the partition stood a pyramid of cans with a sign: SPECIAL TODAY.

Flossie wandered over to the other side of the store. Here she could see a large woman pushing a cart filled with groceries. The woman seemed to be having trouble with the metal cart. Its wheels were worn, and the cart did not move in a straight line.

Flossie giggled to herself as she saw the woman give the handle a sharp tug to set it going forward again. "Maybe I can make it go straight," she told herself.

"I'll push the cart for you," Flossie offered, running up to the annoyed woman.

"Thank you, little girl," the customer said. "It doesn't work very well."

She stepped aside, and Flossie grasped the metal handle. She pushed forward, but the cart turned to the left. With a quick jerk Flossie tried to set it straight. But the cart's wheels turned suddenly to the right, and it hurtled into the pyramid of cans!

Crash! The pile collapsed, and cans rolled in all directions. Nan raced up to Flossie and began to pick up the cans with her small sister.

"What's going on here?" A man in a long white grocer's apron ran into the store through a rear door.

"I'm sorry," Flossie cried, tears in her eyes. "The cart went off the track."

"It wasn't her fault," the woman customer explained. "She was only trying to help me!"

"All right! All right!" The manager helped gather up the fallen cans. "No harm done!"

When they had been built into a pyramid again, and the woman had left, the grocer looked at Nan. "Can I do anything for you?" he asked.

Nan explained about the ice-cream man who had said he was going to pick up some frozen food on Monday. "It was just before one o'clock. Do you remember him?"

"Wore white coveralls, you say?" the grocer repeated. "I'm sure he didn't come in here. I was alone then and would have noticed anyone like that."

Nan thanked the man for the information and Flossie apologized again for the commotion she had caused. Then the two hurried back to school.

Nan reported what they had found out. "It sure looks as if that ice-cream man is the thief!" Bert observed. "I'm going to call Chief Mahoney from the principal's office and tell him!"

The chief himself answered. "No wonder we haven't been able to find that phony electrician if he was wearing a bald wig!" he exclaimed after Bert had told him what the twins had discovered. "Your hunch that it was the ice-cream salesman sounds pretty good."

Before he hung up, the chief added, "I'll send Officer Murphy out to get the piece of wig. We'd better keep it here as evidence."

The children were too excited to continue the puppet rehearsal. They talked to Mr. Tetlow a few minutes, then went outside and sat on the front steps to await Officer Murphy.

Within a short time a police car drove up and the patrolman got out. He came up to the group of children.

"The chief tells me you've found a good clue to the theft of that statuette," he said to Bert.

"Yes," said Bert. "We think the thief was a man who was selling ice cream here Monday noon! He put on a bald wig to disguise himself and then said he was sent to check the lights. But we can't figure out why he wore different colored coveralls."

"Maybe he had on two pairs," the officer suggested. "Anyway, you kids are pretty smart to have figured this out. Now all we have to do is find this ice-cream salesman!"

Suddenly Bert snapped his fingers. "Say! I wrote down the license number of the truck! It's not really his. He rented it for a week."

"We'll find him," the policeman said, and he took out his notebook. "What's the license number?"

Bert put his hand in his pocket. Then he felt hurriedly in all his other pockets. He looked embarrassed. "I don't have the book I wrote it in. It must be at home. I'll get it and call you."

"Okay! I'll take this piece of the wig to headquarters. Keep up the good work!" Officer Murphy grinned at the children and drove off.

Bert was eager to look for his notebook, so the Bobbseys said good-by to Nellie and Charlie and hurried home. When they arrived Flossie whispered something to Freddie, and the small twins ran off to the kitchen.

"You smelled my cookies?" Dinah looked up from her work with a big smile. "I declare to goodness, you children have the sharpest noses in town!"

Flossie giggled. "We really didn't smell them, but we'll eat some! Freddie and I want to ask you something."

Dinah passed the cookies, then motioned to the table. "Sit down and tell me what's on your mind!" she said with a twinkle in her eye. "I can tell you're up to something!"

Freddie and Flossie perched on two stools and took turns telling Dinah about the pet show which they had planned for school. "We need a lot of things. Will you help us, Dinah?" Freddie pleaded.

"I sure will!" the jolly cook replied with a chuckle. "You all just tell me what you want, and I'll get it together for you!"

At that moment Bert came into the kitchen.

"Go away, Bert!" Flossie cried. "Freddie and Dinah and I have a special secret!"

"I'm sorry, but I want to ask Dinah two questions. First, did anyone phone about being Snap's owner?"

"No, Bert," Dinah replied.

"Goody!" cried Flossie.

"Also, Dinah," Bert added anxiously, "have you seen that little brown notebook I had? I've looked all over and can't find it."

"I haven't seen it in the kitchen," Dinah said, "but look out in the garage on the shelf. Maybe you left it there when you cleaned the car yesterday."

"Thanks!" Bert hurried out the back door and into the garage.

Flossie put her lips to Dinah's ear. "We want —" she whispered.

Dinah shook with laughter. "That sounds mighty queer for a pet show," she said, "but I'll put it all in a bag for you to take to school tomorrow."

"Thanks, Dinah," Freddie said solemnly. "This is *very* important!"

"Just you see that I get everything back!" she said as the small twins ran from the room.

In a few minutes Bert returned with a worried look on his face. "It isn't there," he reported. "And I think I *did* leave it on that shelf!"

"Come on, Bert!" Nan called. "Maybe it's upstairs some place. I'll help you look."

They searched thoroughly, but the notebook was not found. "Officer Murphy won't think

I'm such a good detective now!" Bert observed glumly.

"Don't worry about it, Bert," Nan consoled her twin. "I'm sure it'll turn up!"

Mr. and Mrs. Bobbsey were interested to hear about the clue of the wig when Nan told them about it at supper. "I think you children are doing a very good job!" their mother said proudly.

At that moment Snap pushed open the door from the kitchen and walked into the dining room.

"What's that he has in his mouth?" Mr. Bobbsey asked curiously.

"Here, boy!" Bert snapped his fingers. Snap trotted over and laid something on the boy's knee.

It was the missing notebook!

CHAPTER X

PET PRIZES

"SNAP found your notebook for you!" Flossie cried gleefully.

"Good for you!" Bert exclaimed, picking up the little brown book and leaning down to pat the dog. "I wonder where he got it?"

"Snap sleeps in the garage," Nan pointed out. "Maybe he took it off the shelf where you left it!"

"Ask him!" Freddie urged.

Bert grinned. "Snap's smart but he's not *that* smart!"

After supper Bert hurried to the telephone and called police headquarters. Officer Murphy had gone off duty, but the boy left the license number of the truck with the policeman in charge.

"Thanks very much," the officer said. "We'll get busy on this at once."

The pet show which the younger children were putting on was to be the next day. They brought their animals to school with them after lunch.

What a growling, yapping, barking, meowing, and hissing there was as the pupils took their pets to the basement room which had been set aside for the show!

At one end of the room was a small platform with four chairs on it. The children placed the cages and boxes on the tables which lined the sides of the room. Each one was marked with the name of the pet and his owner. Mr. Carter had volunteered to look after the animals until the show began at the close of school.

"I don't think Snap wants to stay inside all afternoon!" Flossie said worriedly. The shaggy dog had been washed the night before, and his coat was white and gleaming.

"Snap won't run away," Freddie assured his twin. "Let him play outside. He'll be good."

The small twins could hardly keep their minds on their studies that afternoon. They kept thinking of the pets. It had been decided that they would put on their act with Susie and Teddy at the beginning of the show.

When school was dismissed at three o'clock,

the four children dashed down to the basement. Flossie brought out a large paper bag which Dinah had given her as they started to school.

With a giggle she passed Teddy two pie pans. "These are the cymbals," she said. "Just bang them together and make lots of noise!"

Freddie reached into the bag and pulled out a series of four bells hung on a braided-silk cord. He struck them with a tiny padded hammer. "Our dinner chimes!" he explained.

Flossie gave Susie a cheese grater and a spoon and took out a glass bottle for herself. "Now, all make a noise together!" she cried.

Teddy banged the pie pans, Freddie struck the bells, Susie ran the spoon over the grater, and Flossie blew across the top of the bottle. What a racket they made!

"That's bee-yoo-ti-ful!" Flossie praised Freddie and the others. "It sounds just like a *real* band!"

Freddie ran outdoors and brought in Snap. Then as soon as the audience had gathered, the four-piece band took chairs. Snap sat on the front of the platform, his tongue hanging out and his tail wagging.

Two boys collected the ten-cent admission fee from everyone. Then Freddie stepped forward and bowed. "I want to introduce Snap, the singing and dancing dog!" he announced proudly.

The little boy sat down, and the children began to play their "instruments." Snap threw back his head and howled. His voice quivered as it ran up and down the scale. The audience clapped loudly.

"More! More!" the children cried when the four stopped playing.

Next Mr. Carter started a small record player which he set on the edge of the platform. At a signal from Freddie, Snap stood on his hind legs. Freddie gave him a rag doll which the dog clasped in his front paws. Then he began to hop around, dancing with the doll!

The children shrieked with laughter. Excited by the noise, Snap hopped faster. When the record ended the dog dropped to all fours again and began to bark as if asking for more music! There were several puppies in the room, and they added their barking and yapping to the chorus.

At a pat from Flossie, Snap stopped barking. The other dogs became quiet too. But suddenly everyone heard one tiny bark. The children looked around.

"That's Archie, my barking frog!" little Ken

Morse piped up. "My grandfather sent him to me from Texas."

Everybody rushed over to look at the frog. He was in a box with a piece of wire netting over the top. The frog was dark brown and about three inches long. His little beady eyes blinked from the top of his wide, flat head.

"Let me see him!" Danny Rugg said, rudely pushing his way in front of the other children. As he did he bumped into the box. The wire lid slid off, and Archie jumped out.

"Oh, catch him!" Ken pleaded.

"I have him!" Bert cried, reaching out for the frog.

But Archie was too quick for him! He leaped from under Bert's fingers and landed on the floor halfway across the room. With another flying leap he reached a window sill. Fortunately the window was closed.

Charlie Mason crept over to the window, his hand cupped. But just as he was about to put his hand over the frog, he jumped again. This time Archie landed in a corner on the floor.

Snap had been watching the commotion, his ears forward and his head cocked to one side. Now he walked slowly over to the corner where the frog lay panting. He put one paw gently on the frog's back.

"He'll hurt Archie!" Ken cried. "Please stop him!"

"Snap won't hurt him," Freddie assured his friend. "He's just holding him for us." With that Freddie picked up the frog and dropped him into his box again. Then he gave Snap an affectionate pat.

"Oh, thank you!" Ken breathed a sigh of relief as he replaced the wire covering. "I wouldn't want anything to happen to Archie!"

Teddy banged the pie pans together, and Freddie stepped up onto the platform. "You may all walk around and look at the animals now. Then the judges will give out the prizes," he announced

Mr. Tetlow, Miss Earle, and Miss Vandermeer had been asked to be judges. They walked slowly around the room, followed eagerly by the pets' owners. As the judges looked at the animals, they made notes on pads of paper they carried.

"I hope they saw Pokey, my turtle," Teddy remarked anxiously. "He likes to hide under the leaves in his box."

"Fluffy is all dressed up," Susie pointed out. "I put a new blue ribbon around her neck." The perky little white kitten sat up in her wire basket looking very content.

Finally Mr. Tetlow and the other judges came back to the platform. Freddie sounded his dinner chimes, and the room grew quiet.

"The judges have agreed on the following awards," the principal said slowly. "The prize for the pinkest nose goes to Peter, Sally Smith's rabbit," he said, holding up a big carrot.

The audience laughed and applauded. Peter twitched his nose.

"And a box of turtle food to Pokey, Teddy

Blake's pet," he continued, "for being the shyest animal in the show!"

Miss Earle stepped up and went on with the prize giving. "Susie Larker's kitten, Fluffy, wins a catnip mouse for being the best behaved," she announced.

Next she awarded dog biscuits to two puppies, one for having the longest ears and the other for the curliest tail.

"Do you s'pose Snap isn't going to get any prize?" Flossie whispered worriedly to Freddie.

"Ssh!" he cautioned. "Mr. Tetlow's going to say something."

The principal raised his hand for silence. "The first prize for talent goes to the Bobbsey twins' dog Snap!" Then while Snap tried to lick the principal's hand, Mr. Tetlow fastened a bright red leather collar around the dog's neck.

"Goody! Goody!" Flossie cried. "Our Snap won first prize!"

"He's the best dog in the whole world!" cried Freddie.

After the show Charlie and Nellie stopped at the Bobbseys' house to congratulate the small twins. "Your band was great!" Charlie said. "Was that your secret?"

Flossie giggled and said, "Yes."

"The whole show was wonderful!" Nan said, hugging her little sister and brother.

"Of course, Danny had to make trouble!" Charlie said in disgust.

"And we haven't thought of any way to pay him back for sending you that note about Snap!" Nellie added.

"Why don't we mail him a frog?" Freddie suggested. "Then when he opened the box, it would jump out at him!"

They all laughed at the picture of Danny's surprise.

But Bert shook his head. "A frog might be too hard to get," he objected. "Let's think of something else."

Nan spoke up. "Danny's always making fun of our solving mysteries. I wish we could trap him that way!"

"I know!" Bert cried. "Let's make him think he can find the missing statue!"

"But how?" Nellie asked. "Even *we* don't know."

Bert thought hard. "Why not write Danny a note telling him he can find the statue at some deserted place?"

Everyone agreed on Bert's plan, and Nellie printed a note which said:

"If you want to show you're a better detective

than the Bobbseys, you can find the missing snake goddess at Jimmy's Drive-In on Route 16." She signed it, "A Friend."

Nan laughed. "That's perfect! I can just see Danny's face when he gets it!"

Charlie and Nellie agreed to mail the note on their way home. "Danny will have it when he goes home to lunch tomorrow!" Charlie said with a chuckle.

That evening Bert had just settled down to study his homework when the telephone rang. Chief Mahoney was calling.

"We've checked that license number, Bert," he reported.

"Whose was it?" Bert asked eagerly.

The chief said that the license had been issued to a car rental agency. Upon checking with the company he learned that the truck had been rented to a man named Ernie Perry.

"Who is he?"

"Well, that's the funny thing about it," the chief said. "Ernie Perry works at the home of Mr. Nelson, the man who owns the statuette!"

CHAPTER XI

A BULLY IS TRICKED

"WORKS for Mr. Nelson!" Bert repeated in amazement. "Then he couldn't be the thief!"

"It does seem strange," Chief Mahoney admitted. "I'll send a detective out to Nelson's house to talk to this Perry. I'll let you know what we find out."

Bert thanked the chief, then went to tell Nan and the small twins the news. They all agreed that it was a very odd situation.

"But if Mr. Perry works for Mr. Nelson, why is he selling ice cream?" Nan asked, perplexed.

Bert shrugged. "Maybe he just wanted to earn a little extra money while Mr. Nelson is away."

The next day at recess Bert asked to see Mr. Tetlow. The secretary spoke to the principal on the telephone, then motioned Bert to go into the private office.

99

Mr. Tetlow looked up with a smile. "Good morning, Bert!" he said cordially. "How is the detective work coming along?"

Bert related what the police had learned about the man on the ice-cream truck. Mr. Tetlow looked startled.

"Can you tell me what Perry looks like, sir?" Bert asked. "Perhaps the ice-cream man really isn't Mr. Nelson's employee."

Mr. Tetlow shook his head regretfully. "I'm afraid I can't help you there, Bert," he said. "I've never seen Ernie Perry."

He explained that his friend Mr. Nelson had often spoken of Perry, who had been a great help to him in looking after his art collection.

"Chief Mahoney is going to talk to him," Bert said. "Maybe that will solve the mystery."

At that moment the bell rang, and Bert hurried back to his classroom. When he went home to lunch he received a telephone call from the police chief.

"Our men couldn't find Perry this morning," the chief explained. "There was no one at the Nelson house. But we'll keep trying," he added before he said good-by.

"I don't think Perry is much of a clue," Bert told Nan. "The disappearance of that statue is as much of a mystery as ever!"

"Don't forget Danny is going to find it for you!" Nan said with a laugh.

"I wonder if he got the letter," Bert replied. "Charlie and I are all ready to follow him on our bicycles if he takes off after school!"

Danny seemed to be in a very good humor that afternoon. He even volunteered to help Miss Vandermeer when she had difficulty opening a window. And every once in a while he would give Bert a triumphant look.

At the end of the school day Danny strolled up to Bert and Nan as they stood on the steps of the building. "I thought you Bobbseys were such good detectives!" he jeered. "You can't even find an old statue that was stolen right under your noses!"

"That's right, Danny!" Bert said cheerfully. Then he winked at Nan. "Maybe you can do better!"

"I just might do that!" Danny returned with a sneer. Then he sauntered off.

Bert caught Charlie's eye, and they watched as Danny went over to the bicycle rack. He pulled his bike out, hopped on, and rode down the driveway. As he turned the corner Bert and Charlie ran to get their bicycles.

"Good luck!" Nan called as they pedaled after the other boy.

"He's headed toward Route 16 all right!" Charlie observed with a chuckle as the boys spotted Danny ahead of them.

"I wish we could be there when he rides up!" Bert said with a grin.

"I think we can!" Charlie observed. "We can take a short cut to Jimmy's Drive-In by going up Elm Street!"

"Okay!" Bert began to pedal faster.

The two boys rode in silence until they were out of town. Then, as they turned onto a road which brought them into Route 16, Bert remarked, "I'm sure we've beaten him!"

Charlie looked back along the highway. There was no sign of the bully. "I hope Danny *is* coming here. The joke would be on us if he doesn't show up!"

"I think he's coming!" Bert assured Charlie. "When he talked to Nan and me, he sounded as if he was sure of finding the snake goddess!"

Jimmy's Drive-In was a circular building with counters all around the outside. The center kitchen section had wooden blinds drawn down over it. Fastened to the building was a large sign reading:

CLOSED FOR THE WINTER
OPEN MAY 15

Bert and Charlie rode up to the deserted restaurant. "Let's hide behind one of these front counters," Bert suggested. "Then we can see Danny when he comes."

"He'll see our bikes!" Charlie pointed out.

"Quick!" Bert exclaimed. "We'll put them back of that little building over there!" He pointed to a dilapidated shack which stood nearby.

The two boys slipped from the seats and stood the bicycles against the far wall of the shack. They could not be seen from the drive-in.

"Hurry! I see someone riding up the highway!" Charlie cried. "It must be Danny!"

The excited chums had just climbed over the front counter and hidden themselves when Danny rode up on his bicycle. He dismounted and peered around uneasily. Then, trying to look unconcerned, he leaned against the counter and stared out at the road.

It was all Bert and Charlie could do to keep from laughing out loud! After a few minutes Danny began to pace up and down. Then he walked around the outside of the building.

Just as he returned to the front, an old car drove up. A rough-looking man got out and walked toward the drive-in restaurant. Danny looked uncertain, but he spoke to the man.

"Do you know where the snake goddess is?" he asked in a shaking voice.

The stranger stopped abruptly and looked at Danny suspiciously. "What you talkin' about, bud?" he asked hoarsely. "I don't know nothin' about no snakes! I just stopped to get a hamburger."

"S-sorry!" Danny stammered. "The r-restaurant's closed!"

With a disgusted look at Danny, the man got back in the car and drove away without a word. This was too much for Bert and Charlie.

They whooped with laughter! Danny jumped
as if he had been stung and looked around at the
counter. The two boys stood up.

"Are you James Smith by any chance?" Bert
asked innocently when he was able to speak.

"You—you!" Danny sputtered. *"You* wrote
that letter!"

"Just answering your note, Danny-boy!"
Bert said with a grin.

Danny's face turned beet-red. He ran over to
his bicycle, jumped on it, and raced down the
road!

"Boy! Did that trick ever work!" Charlie
chortled as Danny disappeared in the distance.

Nan, Nellie, and the small twins were waiting eagerly at the Bobbseys' house for the two
boys. They had a good laugh when Bert and
Charlie took turns telling about Danny's visit
to the drive-in.

"It serves him right," Flossie said stoutly,
"for scaring us about Snap!"

The next day was Saturday and the twins
gathered around the breakfast table a little later
than usual. Nan was glancing at the morning
newspaper. Suddenly she gave an exclamation.

"That circus is in Sanderville!" she cried.

"A circus!" Freddie and Flossie both put
down their spoons. "Wow! Let's go!"

"This is a special circus," Nan replied.

"What do you mean?" Bert asked.

"It's the Hayden Circus!"

"Oh, the one that went off the track just ahead of our train!" Bert exclaimed.

"You mean the one maybe Snap belongs to," Freddie said, his face falling.

Nan read more of the notice in the newspaper. It said that the Hayden Circus had been traveling around the state and would give performances in Sanderville that day.

Mrs. Bobbsey came into the dining room at that moment. Nan showed her the paper. "May we go?"

"We'll see what your father says," she replied. "I really think we should find out, in any case, if Snap belongs to that circus."

"Oh, Mommy, we can't send Snap away!" Flossie wailed.

"But, dear," Mrs. Bobbsey explained, "if he belongs to someone else, we can't keep him."

"Maybe Daddy will buy him for us!" Freddie suggested hopefully.

"We'll see!" his mother said.

Mr. Bobbsey had already left for his office at the lumberyard on the shore of Lake Metoka, so Mrs. Bobbsey telephoned him and explained about the circus.

"Why not take Snap and the children over to Sanderville this afternoon?" he suggested. "And see what you can find out. I'd come too, but I'm very busy here."

He paused a moment, then went on, "I suppose we could try to buy the dog."

"That's what the children were hoping you'd say." Mrs. Bobbsey laughed as she said good-by.

The twins felt happier about taking Snap to Sanderville when their mother told them there was a possibility of her buying the pet.

After an early lunch they all piled into the station wagon. Snap sat on the back seat between Freddie and Flossie, as he had done the first night.

Sanderville was about twenty miles away and considerably larger than Lakeport. When Mrs. Bobbsey reached the outskirts of the city she inquired at a service station about the circus grounds.

"They're over on the other side of town," the attendant informed her. "Go straight through on Main Street. You can't miss the circus. Have a good time!" The children waved happily.

Traffic was heavy at that time of day, and when the Bobbseys reached the circus grounds, the show had started. Mrs. Bobbsey parked the car and asked a guard where they might find the manager. He pointed to a small tent nearby.

Flossie snapped a leash on Snap's collar, and they walked toward the manager's quarters. Sounds of music and clapping came from the main tent.

Mrs. Bobbsey stepped into the manager's office ahead of the children. A short, plump man with a big cigar in his mouth was talking to a man made up as a clown. When the short man saw Mrs. Bobbsey he came forward.

"Are you looking for me, ma'am?" he asked in a pleasant tone. Then he looked beyond her. "Bob!" he exclaimed in astonishment. "Where did you come from?"

CHAPTER XII

A TRIP TO THE MOON

"BOB?" Surprised, Mrs. Bobbsey looked around. Only the twins and Snap were behind her. But Snap was whining eagerly and straining at his leash.

Bert stepped up. "Do you know this dog?" he asked the circus manager.

"Sure!" the man replied. "He's Bob, Red Rankin's trick dog. He disappeared, and we thought he must have been hurt or killed in that train accident."

"But his name's Snap!" Flossie protested. "He followed us home, and he lives at our house!"

The circus man walked over to the dog and put out his hand. Snap licked it eagerly. Then he jumped up and put his front paws on the man's shoulders.

"It's Bob all right, or my name isn't Tiny Hayden!" the fat man declared.

Quickly Mrs. Bobbsey explained that they had been on the train behind the derailed one, and described how the dog had attached himself to their family.

"He's a good dog," Mr. Hayden agreed. "He and Red put on a fine act!"

"May we see this Mr. Rankin, who owns the dog?" Mrs. Bobbsey asked pleasantly.

Mr. Hayden shook his head sadly. "I'm afraid not," he said. "When Bob disappeared, Red's act was gone. He left the circus."

"But you must know where he went!" Nan said in distress.

"No, my dear, I don't!" the circus man replied. "Red was a good boy, but he was getting tired of circus life. He said he thought he'd try something else."

While this conversation had been going on, Freddie and Flossie had been staring at the clown. He had a broad, red mouth painted over his dead-white make-up. Little black spots over and under his eyes made them look very funny.

As the twins watched, he gave them a big wink. "Would you like to peek inside the big tent?" he asked.

The children looked eagerly at their mother. She nodded consent. "Just a peek," she said. "We must be starting home shortly."

After Freddie and Flossie had gone off with the friendly clown, Mr. Hayden pulled several camp chairs forward. "Do sit down," he urged.

Taking a seat, Mrs. Bobbsey asked uncertainly, "What shall we do about the dog? Leave him here?"

Settling into a chair and relighting his cigar, which had gone out, the circus manager puffed for a moment. Then he said, "Your children seem very fond of the dog, and he'll have a good home with you. I suggest that you keep him for the present."

Bert and Nan both smiled. "That sounds like a great idea!" Bert cried. "We'll take good care of Snap."

Mr. Hayden smiled. "And if I hear from Red Rankin, I'll give him your address, and you people can work the problem out between you."

"That's terrific!" cried Nan with pleasure.

Snap seemed to approve of the arrangement. He pranced about and barked happily as Mrs. Bobbsey, Bert, and Nan walked back to the station wagon.

In a few minutes Freddie and Flossie ran up. "Oh, Mommy," Flossie bubbled, "we had the best time! We saw the monkeys and the ponies again. And I'm sure one of the monkeys remembered me! He waved!"

"Maybe he thought you were his sister!" Bert said teasingly.

Flossie made a face at Bert and gave him an impish poke.

Freddie saw Snap stretched out on the back seat of the station wagon. "Is he going home with us?" he asked excitedly.

Bert and Nan explained that they were to keep Snap until Red Rankin claimed him.

Flossie threw her arms about the shaggy dog. "I hope Mr. Rankin has gone to the moon and will never come back for you!" she exclaimed. Snap licked her hand and wagged his fluffy tail in response.

Mrs. Bobbsey threaded her way through the city traffic once more and headed the car toward Lakeport. She was making good time when suddenly a white panel truck turned onto the highway in front of her. She put on the brakes and slowed down. The truck swayed a moment, then picked up speed and raced along the road.

"I think that was the ice-cream man we're looking for!" Nan exclaimed. "I caught only a glimpse of him but I'm sure it was!"

"What's the license number, Bert?" Freddie asked excitedly, standing up and peering through the windshield.

"Can you drive faster, Mother?" Bert urged. "We must catch that man!"

Mrs. Bobbsey speeded up. But the faster she drove, the faster the truck went. Suddenly it careened into a side road. Mrs. Bobbsey was going too fast to turn safely.

"Mother!" Nan exclaimed. "You've lost it!"

Mrs. Bobbsey by this time was entering into the spirit of the chase. Quickly she backed to the side road, turned, and sped down it. The road was narrow and full of holes, and the station wagon bumped and swayed.

Finally she slowed down. "I'm afraid we've

lost the truck, children," she said. "I just can't go any faster on this road. It'll ruin the car."

In spite of the twins' protests she turned the car and drove back to the highway. Later, as they neared the outskirts of Lakeport, Bert turned to his mother. "Let's stop at police headquarters and see if Chief Mahoney has any more news," he suggested.

Mrs. Bobbsey and Snap waited in the car while the four children went into the building. The chief was busy when they arrived, but within a few minutes they were ushered into his office.

The officer smiled when he saw them. "How are the little detectives this afternoon?" he inquired. "Any more clues for me?"

Eagerly Freddie told about the white panel truck which they had seen on the highway. "He was going so fast we couldn't catch him!" the little boy ended his story.

"That's very interesting," Chief Mahoney said. "My men have been watching the Nelson place, and Perry isn't there. They talked to the neighbors and learned that he was planning to take his vacation while Mr. Nelson is in Europe."

The police officer continued, "We've also had a report that a gang of art thieves from New

York has been operating in this area. I'm inclined to believe that the man who stole Mr. Nelson's statuette was a member of that gang."

"You mean you think he probably has left Lakeport by now?" Bert asked.

The chief nodded. "We've sent our report to the New York police and are hoping they'll have some news for us."

The twins turned away, discouraged. It looked as if they were not going to be able to solve the mystery of the snake goddess.

"I'll let you know if we find out anything from New York," the chief called after the twins as they left.

When the station wagon pulled into the Bobbseys' driveway Snap jumped out and ran to the back yard. The twins followed their mother into the house.

"I'm hungry!" Freddie said with a sigh, patting his stomach.

Mrs. Bobbsey smiled. "I think if you go out to the kitchen Dinah might be able to find something for you to eat."

"Sounds like a good idea," Bert observed. "I'll go along!"

"Me too!" both Nan and Flossie cried.

In the kitchen Dinah set a plate of cookies on the table. "You all eat them here," she directed.

"I just finished cleaning the downstairs, and I don't want you all trapsin' around and gettin' a lot of crumbs on my floor."

Bert and Nan took chairs while the small twins perched on the two tall stools. They told Dinah about their visit to the circus.

"Snap's going to live here until Red Rankin gets back from the moon!" Freddie announced.

"Land sakes!" Dinah exclaimed. "What's he doin' on the moon?"

"He's eating lots of green cheese!" Flossie replied with a giggle.

Bert and Nan laughed. "He hasn't really gone to the moon, Dinah," Nan explained. "Flossie just said she wished he *would* go there and not come back for Snap!"

"Oh!" Freddie looked disappointed. He stood up on the rungs of the stool and reached for the cookies. Just as his hand grasped the plate, the stool slipped out from under him. Freddie went down with a crash! The plate fell to the floor and broke, while pieces of cooky scattered in all directions!

Dinah rushed over. "Are you hurt, Freddie?" she asked anxiously.

The little boy shook his head ruefully as Bert helped him up. "No, but I got crumbs on the floor! I'm sorry!"

Flossie picked up the broken plate and the larger pieces of cooky. Nan got the broom and swept up the rest. In a few minutes all was back to normal.

Bert wandered over to the back door and gazed out. "I wonder what Snap has in his mouth," he said. "He's holding something in his teeth and running around the yard like mad!"

"Let's see!" Flossie ran outside, followed by the others.

They laughed when they saw their pet. "It's only a piece of red cloth," Freddie said when the dog had come closer.

Suddenly Snap dashed to the back of the yard, skidded to a stop, turned, and ran back to where the children stood. He shook the cloth with a growling sound, then raced off again!

"Catch him, Bert!" Nan cried.

The next time Snap raced by the twins, Bert reached out and grabbed his collar. "Steady there, old boy!" Bert called. "Let me see that cloth."

With ears pricked up and tail wagging, Snap permitted Bert to take the cloth from his jaws. The boy held it up. It was a square of red silk.

"It looks like a big handkerchief!" Nan exclaimed. "Where do you suppose it came from?"

His fun over, Snap stretched out on the grass,

panting. Dinah had come to the door to watch the excitement.

"Is this yours, Dinah?" Bert asked, showing her the piece of silk.

Dinah shook her head. "It's right pretty," she observed, "but it's not mine. Maybe that man who was here while you all were gone dropped it."

"Who was that?" Nan asked curiously.

The cook explained that a man had come to the back door asking for work. She had suggested he might try at the lumberyard.

"What did he look like?" Freddie wanted to know.

"He was a nice-lookin' man. He had red hair," Dinah replied.

"Red hair!" Bert exclaimed. Then he turned to Nan. "Do you suppose he could have been the circus man, Red Rankin?"

CHAPTER XIII

THE DESERTED HOUSE

NAN looked at Bert in surprise when he suggested that the caller might have been Red Rankin.

"You mean he was here hunting for Snap?" she asked.

"Maybe," Bert replied. "He may have come to Lakeport when he left the circus. Remember, Mr. Hayden said he was going to look for some other kind of work."

Nan was becoming more convinced. "And you think he dropped the handkerchief and Snap recognized it?"

"Dogs can often tell people by their scent," Bert said. "Maybe Snap can trail the man who dropped the handkerchief!"

"Let's try him!" Nan's brown eyes sparkled with excitement.

Bert called to Snap, who rose, stretched, and

walked over to the twins. Holding the piece of red silk to the dog's nose, Bert said, "Get him, boy!"

Snap whined gently but did not move. "Come on," Bert urged. "Find him!"

The dog sniffed at the handkerchief again. Then he started off at a trot, the children behind him.

When Snap reached the street he paused. With a little whimper he ran first in one direction, then another. Finally, as if he had made up his mind, he started down the sidewalk.

"He's going toward the lake!" Freddie exclaimed as Snap made a turn at the next corner.

Lake Metoka, on the edge of Lakeport, was not a long walk from the Bobbseys' house. This was where Mr. Bobbsey's lumberyard was located.

Snap went on, stopping now and then to sniff at a leaf or patch of grass. Finally he reached the shore and turned in the direction of the lumberyard. But before reaching it, Snap turned again and ran to the Bobbseys' boathouse. He stood by the door, whining.

"The man must be in there!" Nan exclaimed.

"Oh, this is 'citing," Flossie cried, taking Nan's hand.

Bert pushed open the door, and Snap dashed

in. He ran to a corner where an old blanket lay.

"Nobody's here!" Flossie said, disappointed.

"Where did the blanket come from?" Nan asked curiously. "I never saw it before!"

"I don't know," Bert replied, "but Snap seems to recognize it!"

The dog pushed the blanket around with his nose. Then he ran from the boathouse onto the dock and stood there barking.

"The man must be here somewhere!" Bert decided. "Let's keep looking."

The twins ran along the shore, peering around the other boathouses as they went. But they saw no one. Finally they gave up.

"Dinah said she told the man to ask for work at Daddy's lumberyard," Flossie reminded the others. "Maybe he's there!"

Mr. Bobbsey was coming from his office when the children ran up to the small building. "Hi, twins!" he called. "I'm just going home. Want a ride?"

"We're looking for Snap's owner," Freddie said seriously. "Did he come here?"

"Maybe I could tell you, if I knew who he is," Mr. Bobbsey said teasingly.

The children told him the story of their trip to Sanderville and about the man who had been looking for work at their house.

"You say he has red hair?" Mr. Bobbsey said thoughtfully. "I did see a red-haired man talking to the yard foreman. I'll ask him."

But when he was questioned, the foreman could give little information. He said the man had asked for work, but when told there was none, he had refused to leave his name and address.

"Then we can still keep Snap," Flossie said as she climbed into her father's car for the trip home. The others happily agreed.

Monday when the twins came back to school after lunch, Tony, the ice-cream man, and his truck were in the driveway.

"Are we glad to see you!" Bert exclaimed. "That man who took your place came only once. And we didn't have any ice cream all last week!"

Tony looked puzzled. "I don't know what happened to him." Then he grinned. "I guess you're ready for some ice cream now. What flavor will it be?"

The children all gave their orders and business was brisk until the bell rang for classes.

That afternoon as the older twins were leaving school Bert pulled Nan aside. "How about walking with me to the Nelson house and looking around? Maybe we can find out whether

Ernie Perry really *is* the ice-cream man."

"All right," Nan agreed. "Wait until I tell Freddie and Flossie that we're not going directly home."

She was back in a minute, and the two set out for the Nelson house. It was about a mile from the school on a shady street. The houses in that section of town were old and large and were set back from the sidewalks in spacious grounds.

"I think this is where Mr. Nelson lives,"

Bert observed, stopping before a white frame house three stories high. It was surrounded by a large lawn and an iron fence. A driveway at the side led back to what had evidently been a barn. Now it was a roomy-looking garage.

"What shall we do now?" Nan asked a little nervously.

"Ring the front doorbell and ask if Mr. Perry is in," Bert replied firmly.

The two children opened the iron gate and walked up the path to the front porch. There was an old-fashioned bell in the middle of the wooden door.

Bert gave it a twist, and they could hear the loud ring. There was no answer. Bert rang again. Still no one came.

"I guess the police are right," Nan remarked. "There's no one here."

"Let's look around a little before we leave," Bert suggested.

The twins circled the house. All the windows were shut tight, and the shades on the second floor were down. The garage doors were closed.

"Come on, Bert," Nan said finally. "We're not learning anything. Let's go home."

The children let themselves out the gate and hurried down the sidewalk. But Nan turned to look back.

"Bert!" she cried. "There's someone at that upstairs window!"

Quickly Bert glanced up. "I don't see anyone," he protested.

"There! Where the window shade is raised." Nan pointed. "He's gone now, but I'm sure I saw a man watching us!"

"That's queer," Bert remarked. "If someone's inside, why didn't he answer the bell?"

"I guess he doesn't want anybody to know he's there," Nan said. The twins, puzzled, went on home.

"We'll come again," Bert declared.

The puppet show had been planned for the next afternoon. When the pupils in Miss Vandermeer's class returned from lunch the teacher announced that Bert, Nan, Nellie, and Charlie would be excused to make their preparations.

As they ran down to the same basement room where the pet show had been held, Bert remarked, "The first thing to do is set up the stage."

Mr. Carter had put a long table on the platform. Now Nan took a length of dark-green cloth from a big box which she and Bert had carried to school at noon.

"Dinah hemmed this for us," she explained to Nellie as the girls began to tack it to the edge of the table. "It will hide us from the audience while we're working the puppets."

Bert and Charlie had fashioned a stage out of cardboard. This they set on the table. Then Bert brought in four little stools from the kindergarten room.

"We can sit on these," he suggested. "I don't think our heads will show above the table."

Nan looked around. "Everything is here except the record player. I'll ask Mr. Carter to get it."

She returned in a few minutes followed by the janitor. He put the record player on the edge of the platform and attached the plug to an electric outlet.

Nan took a record from the box and slipped it on the player. "Mother found this up in the attic!" she said with a laugh. "It's really old!"

"Let's practice once more," Nellie suggested, slipping her fingers into the kitten puppet.

"Okay." Nan put her index finger in the little tube which Bert had fastened to the Ping-pong ball to represent her ostrich's long neck. Her middle finger and thumb went into the wings.

She started the record player and made the ostrich bow low. Just then she heard a groan.

"My clown puppet isn't here!" Bert cried.

"Are you sure?" Nan turned off the record and helped Bert look through the big box. The puppet was gone!

"I was playing with it early this morning," Bert suddenly remembered. "I must have forgotten to put it back in the box!"

"Oh dear!" Nellie exclaimed. "It's almost time for the show to begin!"

"I'll run home and get it," Bert decided. "You'll have to entertain the audience until I get back!" He dashed from the room.

The other three children looked at one another in dismay. What could they do?

Then Nan had an idea. "Let's start off with a sing! We can keep that going until Bert gets back!"

Charlie and Nellie agreed. "You lead it, Nan," Nellie suggested.

The ring of the dismissal bell echoed through the building. Then came the sound of doors opening and a rush of footsteps.

"Here they come!" Charlie cried as the door of the room burst open.

When the children had taken their seats and the admission price had been collected, Charlie stepped forward. "We'll begin by singing a few songs," he announced. "Nan Bobbsey will lead us!"

"Let's have a round," Nan proposed. "The children on the left side of the room will sing 'Three Blind Mice' and those on the other side 'Row, Row, Row Your Boat.' "

The audience entered into the spirit, and soon everyone was singing gaily. Little Teddy Blake could not quite keep up with the others. His piping voice was always a few beats behind!

"That's wonderful!" Nan said when the round came to an end. "What shall we sing now?"

" 'Old MacDonald Had a Farm'!" one of the older boys called out.

This song was a popular one with all the children. They had great fun making all the funny farm noises. Teddy Blake made up for his slowness in the other song by an especially loud *oink, oink!*

Just as the list of animals on MacDonald's farm had been completed, Bert slipped into the room. He held up a package for Nan to see.

She looked relieved. When the final note of the song had died away, Nan held up her hand.

"And now," she announced, "we will have a performance by those world-famed actors, the Lakeport Puppets!"

CHAPTER XIV

THE SHOW GOES ON

"YEA! The Lakeport Puppets!" the children called.

Nan took her place with the other three on the stools behind the table. The next minute four little figures popped up on the stage.

There was a clown in his red-and-white suit. A blue-coated policeman with a tiny club came after him. The ostrich had a rhinestone collar, and as her head bobbed the long eyelashes seemed to flutter. The little kitten was white, and around her neck hung a perky blue ribbon with a bell.

All the puppets made deep bows in response to the applause from the audience. Then the kitten and the ostrich disappeared.

The policeman turned to the audience. "Do you like puzzles?" he asked in a funny deep voice.

"Yes! Yes!" came the shouted replies.

The policeman put one little hand up to his mouth and pretended to whisper to the audience. "I'll ask this clown some and see if he knows the answers!"

The children giggled.

"Now, sir," the policeman said to the clown, shaking his stick, "what has a face but no head, hands but no feet, yet travels all the time and is usually running?"

The clown put his hands up to his head as if in deep thought. Then a card with the word CLOCK printed on it was raised behind him.

"Clock!" the children in the audience shouted.

The clown repeated the word in a squeaky voice.

"You heard!" the policeman objected and beat the clown on the head with his club.

The audience shrieked with laughter.

"I'll give him another chance," the policeman said to the children. Turning to the clown, he asked, "When is a boat like a heap of snow?"

The clown repeated the question in his squeaky voice and again put his hands to his head.

WHEN IT IS ADRIFT appeared on a card held over his head.

Once more the audience called out the answer, and the clown repeated it. The policeman seemed to be beside himself with anger. He paced up and down, shaking his stick and muttering.

Then he stopped and turned to the audience. "Once more!" he said. Facing the clown, he said very slowly, "What animal took the most luggage into the ark?"

Again a card was raised behind the clown's back. This time it said, THE ELEPHANT TOOK A TRUNK.

When the audience called out the answer, the policeman did not give the clown a chance to speak. He hit him on the head and dragged him from the stage.

There was loud applause. The clown and the policeman popped up again and bowed deeply. When the clapping died down, they disappeared and two more figures sprang up. They were the ostrich and the kitten.

"Meow!" the kitten said. The little children in the audience giggled. "My friend Miss Ostrich will sing for you!"

Bert, who had come out from behind the table and taken a seat in the front row, got up and started the record player. The strains of "Down by the Old Mill Stream" floated out over the audience.

Nan, working the ostrich puppet, made her move with the music and appear to be singing. On the high notes the ostrich would fling back her head and open her wings wide.

Danny Rugg, who was seated in the front row, crossed his legs. In doing so, his foot hit the edge of the platform where the record player was. The blow made the needle skip, and part of the song was lost.

Surprised, Nan forgot for a moment to move the puppet. Someone in the audience laughed. Bert replaced the needle with a frown at Danny.

But the laughter had given Danny an idea. Once more he kicked the platform; the needle slid over the record, and the song stopped.

"Please, don't joggle the platform, Danny," Bert protested. "You're spoiling everything!"

"I can't help it if your old platform is rickety!" Danny said rudely. "I have to move my feet!"

Once more Bert set the needle on the record, and the song continued. Then when the singer reached a high note Danny joggled the platform again. The needle slid off, making a screeching sound. But this time Nan picked up the song where it had been stopped and continued in her own voice.

As the song ended, Mr. Tetlow, who had been watching from the back row, walked up to Danny. "You're causing a disturbance here," he said sternly. "I suggest you leave."

There was silence as Danny got up and stalked out of the room. Then the ostrich and the kitten put on a little dance which drew loud applause. At the end the clown and the policeman appeared again, and the four little puppets did a bouncing jig before making their bows of farewell.

When the applause had stopped, Mr. Tetlow stepped to the platform. "I know you will all be interested to know that between the pet show held last week and this puppet performance, the sum of twenty dollars has been raised for the school museum!"

There were cheers and whistles. Then the principal went on, "I shall appoint a committee of teachers and pupils to select something for our exhibits. But today I want to thank those children who worked so hard to make these two affairs the successes they have been!"

There was more applause, and then the audience filed from the room.

"You were awf'ly good puppets!" Flossie said admiringly as she and Freddie joined the older children, who were packing their puppets and the scenery into the big box once more.

"Thank you, honey," Nan said, giving her little sister a hug.

Almost everyone had left the school by the time the puppeteers were ready. "I'll help carry the box, Bert," Charlie offered.

"Okay, take the other end," Bert directed, and the two boys started toward the Bobbseys' home. Nan, Nellie, and the small twins followed.

"I didn't know ostriches could sing, Nan!" Freddie commented as they walked along.

"Ostriches stick their heads in the ground and think no one can see them!" Flossie volunteered. "Miss Earle said so!"

"Like this?" Freddie ran to the soft ground at the side of a low hedge and stood on his head.

As he stayed there waving his legs in the air, Nan noticed an elderly man down on his knees weeding a flower bed on the other side of the hedge.

"Be careful, Freddie!" she cautioned. "You'll fall!"

"Ggl," Freddie replied, his face getting redder by the second.

The next instant he lost his balance and tumbled over the hedge right on top of the man!

"Oh!" Nan cried, jumping over the hedge and

helping Freddie to his feet. "I'm very sorry," she said to the man. "My little brother didn't see you there! I hope you're not hurt!"

Slowly the man got to his feet. Then he stood

still, both hands holding his back. "I guess I'm all right," he said finally, straightening up. "But," he added, "it's rather a surprise to have a small boy land right on your back when you're weeding your garden!"

Freddie looked sheepish. "I was being an ostrich and putting my head in the ground. No one was supposed to see me!"

The man smiled. "Well, I didn't see you, but you'd better look around before you play ostrich."

Freddie promised that he would. Seeing that the man was not hurt, the children resumed their walk. Bert and Charlie were far ahead and had stopped at a corner to wait for the others.

"Freddie was playing ostrich and fell down!" Flossie reported when they reached the boys.

At that moment Danny Rugg rode by on his bicycle. He stopped and waited until the children reached him.

"You think you're smart because you got old Tetlow to send me out of the room," he said with a glare at Bert.

"I had nothing to do with it!" Bert replied. "It was your own fault!"

"Well, you'll be sorry!" Danny called as he mounted his bicycle and rode away.

Bert looked disgusted. "I wonder what he'll try now!"

"Don't pay any attention to him," Charlie advised. "We can take care of Danny Rugg any day!"

"Okay! See you tomorrow!" Bert called as Charlie and Nellie turned down at the next street to go to their homes.

When the twins reached the Bobbseys' house no one was there. "Where is everbody?" Flossie asked in surprise when their calls brought no response.

"Mother had to go to a meeting," Nan replied, "but Dinah should be here."

Just then they heard the back door slam.

They ran to the kitchen. Dinah had evidently just come in. She was puffing and looked worried.

"What's the matter?" Nan asked her.

Dinah replied with another question. "Was Snap at school with you children?"

"Why, no."

"Then I don't know where he is! He's been gone all afternoon!"

CHAPTER XV

A REWARDING SEARCH

"SNAP gone!" Flossie wailed. "Oh, do you s'pose that Red Rankin came and took him away?"

"I don't know," Nan replied. Then she turned to Dinah and asked, "When did you last see Snap?"

Dinah had dropped into a chair and was fanning herself. "He was in the back yard when you all went to school after lunch. Then the next time I looked he wasn't there. I called and called, but he didn't come. I been out huntin' for him. I hoped maybe he'd gone to school to meet you all."

"I'm sure he wasn't at school," Bert said in a worried tone, "or we'd have seen him."

"Let's scout around the neighborhood," Nan suggested. "Snap may be playing with some other dogs."

Nan and Flossie went in one direction while Bert and Freddie walked the other way. They hurried along the street calling their pet. But there was no answer from the shaggy white dog.

Finally the discouraged twins met back at the house. "I can't understand it," Nan said. "Snap has never run away before!"

"Maybe he's gone back to the boathouse!" Freddie suddenly cried.

"That's a thought, Freddie!" Bert started off on a run. The others followed.

But when they reached the boathouse, there was no sign of Snap. The blanket still lay in the corner and appeared to be undisturbed.

Flossie's eyes filled with tears. "Snap's gone, and I'll never see him again!" she cried.

Nan put an arm around her little sister. "I'm sure Snap will come back," she said consolingly. "Don't worry!"

Sadly the twins walked home. When their parents heard the story of Snap's disappearance, Mr. Bobbsey telephoned the police and reported the missing dog.

"If Snap doesn't come back in a day or two, we'll put an ad in the paper," he promised the children.

They tried to be content with this, but before going to bed, Bert and Nan made another tour of the neighborhood calling their pet. The dog did not come.

Freddie woke up early the next morning. "I think I hear Snap!" he told himself.

The little boy quickly put on his robe and slippers and pattered downstairs. Hopefully he pushed open the back door. He was just in time to see a small black dog run out of the yard.

When he turned around he found Flossie close behind him. "I thought I heard Snap," he explained.

"So did I," his twin said. Freddie told her about the black dog, and the two sadly mounted the stairs again.

Later that afternoon when school was over, Bert went up to Charlie Mason. He told his chum about Snap's disappearance.

"I think I'll ride around on my bike and look for him. Want to come along?" he asked.

"Sure!" Charlie agreed. The two boys mounted their bicycles and rode off.

For an hour they went up one street and down another searching for the white dog. When Bert saw a boy he knew standing on a corner, he stopped and described Snap. "Have you seen a dog like that around here?" he asked.

"I did see one that sounds like him," the boy admitted. "But a kid had him on a leash. He went in that house over there." He pointed down the street.

Bert looked at the house and frowned. Then he thanked the boy and rejoined Charlie, who had been waiting for him farther up the street.

Bert told Charlie what the boy had said. "And the house he pointed out is where Jack Westley lives!" he ended angrily.

"I'll bet Danny and Jack took Snap!" Charlie exclaimed. "Let's go get him!"

The two boys parked their bicycles in front of the Westleys' house and rang the doorbell. Mrs. Westley answered.

"Jack's out with his new dog," she said, smiling, when Bert asked for him.

"Do you know where he got the dog?" Charlie inquired casually.

"Oh, yes," Mrs. Westley replied. "He bought him from a friend at school."

The boys thanked Jack's mother and walked away.

"A likely story!" Bert muttered to Charlie as they hopped on their bicycles. "The 'friend' was probably Danny!"

"Let's ambush Jack!" Charlie proposed. "We can hide behind those bushes across the street and grab Snap when Jack comes along with him."

"Okay!"

The two boys looked around. The street was deserted. They rode across to a clump of shrubbery in front of an empty house. Carefully they hid the bicycles and crouched down behind the bushes. They had a clear view up and down the street.

Bert and Charlie had been there only a few minutes when Charlie whispered, "Here they come now!"

About a block away were a boy and a large white dog. The boys watched as they approached. Suddenly Bert gave a groan. "That's not Snap!" he exclaimed. "That dog has short hair!"

Charlie chuckled. "I hope Jack goes into his house and doesn't see us hiding here!"

Jack was paying no attention to anything but his new pet. Whistling to the dog, he ran around the side of the house and disappeared. Cautiously, Bert and Charlie got on their bicycles and rode off.

"We're near the Nelson house," Bert observed. "Let's ride past it." He told Charlie about the face in the window which Nan had thought she saw when they had been there before.

"Sounds spooky!" Charlie commented.

In a few minutes they were passing the old house. Bert looked at the windows. All the shades on the second floor were down. Then he glanced at the garage.

"Say!" he cried, putting on his brake. "The garage door's open, and I think there's a white panel truck parked in there!"

"The same one that was at school?" Charlie asked excitedly.

"I'm going to find out!" Bert jumped off his bicycle and began to walk up the driveway. When he reached the garage, he took out his notebook and compared the license number of the truck with the one he had jotted down at school. It was the same!

He ran down the drive and told Charlie. "I must get to a telephone and call Chief Mahoney right away!" he decided. "Perry must be the ice-cream man! I hope he doesn't leave before the police can get here!"

"I'll stay," Charlie volunteered, "and watch the garage. I'll follow him if he leaves!"

"Good!" Bert jumped on his bicycle and ped-aled off as fast as he could.

There were no stores around this residential district, but after a few minutes Bert spotted a sidewalk phone booth. Quickly he dialed police headquarters.

"Patrolman Murphy and another man will be right over!" the chief assured him when Bert had told his story.

Bert hurried back to the spot where he had left Charlie. No one was there! Then he heard a *pst!* and looked around. Charlie beckoned to him from behind a large tree.

"I decided I'd better get out of sight," Charlie explained. "Someone might see me watching the house."

"The police will be here in a few minutes," Bert assured him. "Then we'll see if Perry is in there."

He had just finished speaking when a police car slid to a stop on the other side of the street. Two officers got out followed by Nan, Freddie, and Flossie.

Seeing Bert's surprise, Nan said with a laugh, "You didn't think you could do this alone, did you?"

Officer Murphy spoke up. "If there's going to be a capture, we thought the other Bobbsey twins should be in on it. We stopped at your house and picked them up."

Bert grinned at his brother and sisters. Then he asked the policeman, "What's the next step?"

"You children stay here on the sidewalk while Kelly and I go up to the house," Officer Murphy directed. "I don't want you in any danger."

The twins and Charlie watched as the police officers walked up to the door of the old house. They rang the bell several times without getting any response.

Then Officer Murphy pounded on the door and called out, "Open up! This is the police!"

Suddenly Flossie shouted, "There goes someone!" She dashed up the walk to the two officers. "I saw a man run away from the back of the house. He's in the garage!" Flossie cried, panting.

By this time the other children had caught up with Flossie. Motioning them to stay behind, the policemen started toward the garage. As they approached the old barn, there was a roar, and the truck motor started up.

"Halt!" Murphy shouted, running into the garage.

In his haste to get the truck running, the driver stalled the motor. At the sight of the police, he shrugged and climbed out of the vehicle.

"What's the big idea?" he blustered. "I've got a right to leave this place if I want to!"

Officer Murphy called the children. "Have you seen this man before?" he asked them.

"Yes!" they chorused, and Nan said, "It's the ice-cream man!"

The officer turned to the man. "What's your name?" he asked.

"Ernie Perry. I work for Mr. Nelson, who lives in this house," he said defiantly.

"Then what are you doing with this truck, and where is the statuette you stole from the school?" Murphy asked sternly.

"I don't know anything about any statuette!" Perry insisted. "I was just trying to make a little money by selling ice cream while my boss is away. There's no law against that, is there?"

"Open up the truck!" Officer Murphy said. "We'll take a look around for that statuette."

"I'll have to go in the house and get the key," Perry said sullenly.

"Maybe not," the policeman said. "Try that one on your key ring!"

With a glare at the smiling officer, Perry unlocked the back of the truck. "Go ahead!" he snarled. "Look until you're blue in the face! You won't find anything!"

The two officers searched the truck carefully. They found nothing except a small supply of paper spoons.

"Satisfied?" Perry asked with a sneer.

CHAPTER XVI

A VALUABLE FIND

"THE snake goddess must be in the truck!"
Bert said desperately.

The officers examined the vehicle again. Still
they did not uncover anything suspicious.

"I told you there was nothing hidden!" Perry
said triumphantly. "I don't know why these kids
are picking on me!"

Bert did not know what to think. Perhaps
Perry was not the thief after all! The embarrassed boy was about to walk out to his bicycle
when he had a sudden thought. He stood back
of the truck and studied it closely. Then he
whispered something to Officer Murphy.

"You're right, Bert!" the policeman exclaimed. "I don't know why I didn't think of
that!"

He motioned to the other officer. "Come on,
Kelly," he called. "Let's pry up the floor of this
truck!"

Ernie Perry turned pale. "You can't do that!" he protested. "You'll ruin the truck!"

"Okay," the policeman said. "If you don't want us to do it, take up that false bottom yourself!"

Still protesting, Perry pushed two concealed buttons, then lifted a portion of the truck's flooring. Beneath it was a space filled with packages.

"Good!" Officer Murphy said. "Now we'll

make sure that you don't leave us suddenly!" He took a pair of handcuffs from his pocket, fastened one end to Perry's wrist and the other to a support in the doorway of the garage.

Then the police officers began to remove the packages from the bottom of the truck. In a few minutes there were six spread out on the grass next to the driveway.

"Is the snake goddess there?" Nan asked eagerly.

"We'll see!" Murphy picked up a brown paper bag and peered into it. He handed the package to Bert, who opened it quickly.

"It's the statuette!" he cried happily.

Perry smirked. "I know valuable art when I see it," he boasted. "That's the best thing Mr. Nelson ever bought! It belongs to him. I didn't steal it for myself." The others doubted this.

"What's in the other packages?" Flossie asked curiously.

While the children watched with interest, the bags were opened. All contained Greek art objects. There were two vases. One of them was like the vase in the school museum collection.

"That's an amphora!" Freddie announced. He was very proud that he had remembered the name Mr. Tetlow had told the children.

The remaining three objects were ornamental

gold cups with designs hammered into the sides. Nan exclaimed, "How lovely!"

"Those are Vaphio gold cups!" Perry told her. "They were made in Crete thousands of years ago. And they are Mr. Nelson's. I was afraid to leave them in the house with nobody home, so I carried them around with me."

Officer Murphy scowled. "I believe they were stolen from the museum at Sanderville!" he said. "It wasn't a gang from New York taking all the art objects around this area. It was you!"

Ernie Perry shrugged his shoulders. "You have no proof."

"Maybe we have," Bert spoke up. "You put on a bald wig and pretended to be an electrician when you took the statuette from school."

The suspected man looked surprised but said nothing. He took a stick of gum from his pocket and began to unwrap it nervously.

Flossie watched with interest and suddenly spoke up. "That's the same kind of gum wrapper Freddie found in the museum room."

Perry glared at the little girl. Officer Murphy was about to say something when Freddie cried, "Here's the wig!"

The little boy had climbed into the truck and searched in the corners under the floor. Now he held up a piece of a bald wig!

"I guess that's proof enough," said the officer. Perry slumped to the ground, too weak to stand. In a trembling voice he confessed everything.

"How did you expect to dispose of all this valuable stuff?" Murphy asked him.

The thief explained that he had a friend in the West who planned to sell the things to a small museum. "We'd have had a good thing going if these kids hadn't snooped around!" he said fiercely.

"That's right!" Officer Murphy agreed. "It's lucky they did."

"We wouldn't have done if it you hadn't been so mean to our dog Snap!" Freddie spoke up.

"Your dog Snap!" Perry repeated scornfully. "You mean the mutt that jumped up on the seat after me? That was Bob, Red Rankin's trick dog!"

"How did you know that?" Bert asked, puzzled.

"I worked at the Hayden circus before I went with Mr. Nelson. That dog never liked me, and I never liked him!"

Officer Murphy motioned to the other policeman. "Come on, Kelly, we'll put these things in the trunk of our car and take them down to headquarters along with Perry."

Bert looked pleadingly at the officer. "Do you think I could take the snake goddess back to school? After all, I'm responsible for it, and I'd like to see it safe in the museum."

The officer patted Bert on the back. "You've done a good job catching this fellow. I think we can let you take the statuette. I'll explain to Chief Mahoney."

Bert's face shone. "Thanks a million, Officer Murphy!" he cried. He carefully rewrapped the little figure in the paper and placed it in the basket on the handlebars of his bicycle.

"May we get out at school too?" Flossie asked as she, Nan, and Freddie climbed into the police car.

"Yes, let's!" Nan said eagerly. "I'd like to see Mr. Tetlow's face when Bert gives him the snake goddess!"

By this time Bert and Charlie had ridden off on their bicycles. "We'll take Perry to headquarters first, then drop you children at the school," Officer Murphy decided as he drove away from the Nelson house.

Bert and Charlie had just arrived at the school building when the police car drew up and the other children jumped out.

"It's pretty late," Bert observed. "I hope Mr. Tetlow is still here!"

The principal was still in his office working on some reports when the five children walked in. He looked up in surprise.

"Well, what brings you to school so late?" he asked, taking off his glasses and leaning back in his chair.

Bert's voice shook with excitement as he cried, "We've brought the statuette!"

Mr. Tetlow jumped to his feet. "You have?" he exclaimed. "Where did you find it?"

When the story of Ernie Perry had been told, the principal looked amazed. "So it *was* Mr. Nelson's man after all!" he exclaimed. "Of course, he would know the value of the museum pieces!"

"And he was the pretend 'lectric light man!" Flossie piped up.

Mr. Tetlow smiled at her. "Without you Bobbsey twins," he said solemnly, "I doubt if we could have recovered the statuette so quickly. I'm certainly very happy to have it back."

"May we put it in the museum again?" Nan asked.

"By all means," Mr. Tetlow replied. "And I'm sure Mr. Carter will take special care of it!"

So the little figure was once more placed on

the shelf in the museum room. Bert heaved a sigh of relief as the children left the school.

"Boy! Am I glad that mystery is solved!" he said thankfully.

"And now if we could only find Snap!" Flossie sighed.

"And his owner!" Freddie reminded her. "Then maybe Daddy could buy Snap for us!"

The twins waved good-by to Charlie and turned toward home. "Want a ride?" Bert asked Flossie.

When the little girl said, "Yes," Nan lifted her into the basket on her brother's bicycle. Flossie was a bit big for the basket even though she sat with her knees up under her chin.

"You're getting big!" Bert teased her as he pretended to puff and pant with the effort of pedaling. "Sit still, or I'll dump you off!"

Flossie giggled. She sat very quietly for a few minutes. Then she saw Susie Larker. Susie had her white kitten on a leash and was walking along the sidewalk on the other side of the street.

Forgetting she was on a bicycle, Flossie turned quickly to get a better look at the strange sight. At the same moment Bert hit a hole in the pavement and lost his balance.

Crash! The bicycle fell to the street and Bert

and Flossie were thrown off! When Bert got un-
tangled from the wheel he ran over to his little
sister, who was seated on the curbstone rub-
bing her knee.

"Are you all right, Flossie?" Bert asked anxiously, kneeling down beside her.

"I—I guess so!" Flossie quavered. "But I

skinned my knee!" A few tears welled up in her blue eyes.

At that moment Nan and Freddie ran up. They had seen the spill from a distance. Nan took Flossie's hand. "Come on, honey," she said comfortingly. "We'll hurry home and fix your knee."

By the time Flossie's knee was bandaged, Dinah was sounding the dinner chimes.

When the Bobbseys had gathered around the supper table, Bert told his exciting story.

"I'm proud of you all!" Mr. Bobbsey said when his son had finished. "You did very well to solve the mystery of that stolen statue!"

Just then a shrill whistle sounded. Everyone stopped talking and listened. Then two more whistles came.

"It's a fire!" Freddie shouted, springing from his chair.

As the others jumped up too, they heard the clang of fire engines rushing down the street. Bert ran to the window. A glare lighted the sky.

"I think it's near the lake, Dad!" Bert cried.

Mr. Bobbsey dashed to the telephone and called the firehouse. His face was white when he turned back to his family.

"Our boathouse is on fire!" he said grimly.

CHAPTER XVII

HELPING THE FIRE FIGHTERS

"OUR boathouse!" Bert repeated in horror. "Your boats, Dad, and my canoe will be ruined!" He dashed toward the door.

"I'll put out the fire!" Freddie shouted, running after his brother. "Let me get my pumper!" Freddie loved playing fireman and had an engine that sprayed real water.

"Just a minute!" Mr. Bobbsey called. "I'm not sure you children should go down there! It may be dangerous!"

"Oh, please, Daddy!" Nan begged. "It's *our* boathouse that's on fire!"

"They can stay in the station wagon with me, Dick," the twins' mother suggested.

"Very well," Mr. Bobbsey relented. "We'll all go. You may be able to help, Bert. The wood in our boathouse has been treated and will resist fire for a short time."

157

When the children and their parents had finally piled into the car, the streets were full of people hurrying toward the lake front. As another fire engine roared past, the glow in the sky grew redder.

"Hurry, Daddy!" Freddie urged, standing up and leaning over his father's shoulder.

Mr. Bobbsey drove as fast as he dared through the increasing traffic. When they were half a block away from a busy intersection, the Bobbseys heard a loud *crash!*

"What happened?" Flossie cried.

"That hook and ladder that just passed us has hit something!" Bert exclaimed.

Mr. Bobbsey stopped the station wagon, and they all ran up to the intersection. The hook and ladder had struck a parked car and skidded across the street, completely blocking it!

"We have to get to the fire, Daddy!" Freddie cried desperately. "How can we pass?"

By that time the firemen and several passers-by were surveying the wreck. The rear bumper of the car had caught under the front of the fire truck, and the driver of the hook and ladder could not back away!

"I think we can lift this car from under the truck," Mr. Bobbsey observed. At his direction two men stood on the bumper while he and two of the firemen pulled the car loose. Then with a wave of thanks the firemen backed the truck and clanged away toward the lake. The Bobbseys ran back to their car.

Once more they sped on their way. But they had just passed the intersection when the station wagon suddenly slowed down, then stopped.

"Oh, oh," Mr. Bobbsey exclaimed. "We're out of gas!"

A police car pulled alongside. Officer Murphy was driving. "Something wrong?" he called out.

"We're going to the fire!" Freddie said anxiously. "It's our boathouse! But we're out of gas!"

"All of you get in my car," the officer urged. "I'll take you to the lake!"

When they reached the waterfront, the children gasped. Not only was the Bobbseys' boathouse on fire, but several others on one side of it were blazing.

The wind had increased, and red sparks crackled up into the evening sky. Water from three engines poured onto the flames. The firemen worked furiously, hacking through windows and spraying chemicals onto fuel tanks to keep them from exploding.

Every few minutes there would be a great

hissing sound and more white smoke would billow forth from the boathouses. A large crowd had collected and stood silently watching.

As Officer Murphy's car came to a stop, one of the firemen hurried over. Recognizing Mr. Bobbsey, he shook his head sympathetically. "I hope you haven't any valuable boats in there!" he said. "This fire's pretty bad!"

"Three of them!" Mr. Bobbsey replied grimly, getting out of the car. He looked toward his large boathouse. "The fire seems to be on just the left side," he observed. "I'll see if I can save one of the boats anyway!"

"I'll help!" Bert volunteered, climbing out after his father.

"Me too!" Freddie called.

"No," Mr. Bobbsey said firmly. "You and the girls stay here with your mother! Bert and I will see what we can do!"

The firemen were reluctant to allow Mr. Bobbsey and Bert through the lines, but finally agreed to let them try to save at least one of their boats.

At that moment two men who worked at the lumberyard ran up. "We'll get the big boat out!" one of them cried.

"Good!" Mr. Bobbsey agreed. "Bert and I will try to rescue the other two!"

Quickly the men ran the lumber launch out into the lake. Mr. Bobbsey jumped into his motorboat and started the engine. It roared to life.

"Paddle down the lake!" he yelled to Bert, who was already in his canoe. "Pull in at the first dock, and I'll meet you there!"

The wall next to Bert was ablaze and the heat was almost unbearable. The boy wasted no time. Paddling with all his might, he reached the cool air of the lake. He wiped his moist forehead and breathed a sigh of relief. But as he paddled past the burning boathouse next door, a large spark fell into the canoe. It landed on a cushion which had been left in the bow. The cloth began to burn.

"I'll have to put that out!" Bert thought desperately. Carefully putting his paddle on the bottom of the canoe, and holding onto the gunwales, he inched his way forward. The craft rocked dangerously.

Finally the boy could stretch out one hand and grasp an edge of the cushion. With a quick motion he tossed it overboard!

"Whew!" Bert gasped when he was safely in his seat again. "That was a close one!"

A few minutes later he joined his father and the two lumberyard workmen at the dock. They had tied up their boats and now pulled Bert's canoe up on the shore.

"Good work, son!" Mr. Bobbsey said, patting Bert on the back.

"We're lucky we could save all the boats!" the boy observed happily.

Mr. Bobbsey gazed back toward the fire. "And just in time, I'd say! Those firemen have a fight on their hands!"

When Bert and his father got back to the blazing buildings, one of the firemen spoke to them. "Glad you got those boats out," he said. "The fire in your boathouse is almost out, but the wind has carried sparks over to others nearby. We've sent for another engine from the next town!"

For a while the Bobbseys stood in silence, watching the yellow flames against the dark sky. Then the engine from the neighboring town arrived and more giant hoses sent out gushes of water. With this added help, the fire was gradually brought under control.

Finally all but one of the engines left. It continued to throw water on the smoldering buildings. The crowd began to drift away as the excitement died down.

"Where's Freddie?" Mr. Bobbsey asked suddenly.

Mrs. Bobbsey pointed over toward the remaining fire engine. There was Freddie, deep in conversation with a fireman.

The little boy told the man who he was and that he hoped to become a fireman when he grew up.

"I wish I could squirt some water on this fire," he added wistfully.

The fireman smiled. "Well, since you're going to work with us some day," he said, "maybe we could let you show us how good a fireman you are."

Freddie beamed up at the tall fire fighter. "You mean it?" he asked in delight.

"Sure I do." The man in the rubber coat and hat took the little boy by the hand. "Come with me," he said.

They walked over to another fireman, who was playing a stream of water on the roof of one of the boathouses. "I have a helper for you, Mac!" Freddie's friend said. "He'd like to help spray that roof!"

"Okay!" Mac replied with a grin. He placed Freddie's hand on the nozzle of the big hose.

The hose was heavy, so the fireman held it steady while Freddie directed the water toward the boathouse roof.

"This is great!" Freddie was thrilled to

think that he was helping to put out a real fire! Once in a while he would look around to see if anyone was watching him.

Finally the first fireman said, "That's fine, but maybe you'd better run back to your father now. I see he's looking for you!"

Freddie thanked his new friend and returned to the police car. He was just telling his family about the exciting adventure when the fire chief walked up.

"Do you know what could have started the

fire, Mr. Bobbsey?" he asked. "Was anyone in your boathouse this afternoon?"

"Not that I know of," the twins' father replied. "Did the fire actually start there?"

"Looks like it. My men examined the place when they first got here. They found a partly burned blanket in one corner of the side that was blazing and sending out sparks. A lighted match falling on it could have started the whole thing."

"I haven't used any of the boats for several days," Mr. Bobbsey said. "Perhaps some prowler broke into the boathouse!"

The twins looked at one another, and the same thought crossed their minds. Could Red Rankin have been the one to set the boathouse on fire?

Before they could say anything, the chief held out a battered-looking book. "Ever see this before?" he asked.

Bert gasped. It was a school geography book!

"Where did this come from?" he asked.

"We found it right outside your boathouse."

"May I look at it?" Bert asked. He took the book and opened the cover.

"Whose is it?" Nan asked curiously.

Bert held the book so that the car's headlights shone on it. "Danny Rugg's!" he exclaimed.

"But how did Danny's book get by our boathouse?" Nan asked in bewilderment.

"Search me!" Bert shrugged.

"There's Danny now!" Flossie cried out, pointing to a group of boys standing around the remaining fire engine.

"Ask him to come over here, will you, Bert?" the fire chief directed. "I'd like to talk to him."

Bert walked over to where Danny and Jack Westley were talking to a fireman. When Bert relayed the chief's message, Danny said nervously, "Why does he want to see me?"

"He found your geography book outside our boathouse," Bert said. "He—"

"I don't know anything about any book, and I'm not going over there!" Danny said rudely. He turned to walk away.

When Bert put out his hand to stop the bully, Danny gave him a hard shove. Bert tripped over a fire hose and fell backward with a thud! Danny ran off laughing.

CHAPTER XVIII

AN EXCITING SALE

NAN saw Bert fall. She started forward as Danny ran off. "Don't let him get away!" she cried as her twin struggled to his feet.

"We'll catch him!" Freddie and Flossie called, racing after Danny. Bert and Nan joined in the chase. The next minute Danny stumbled over a hose himself and fell to the ground.

"Listen," Bert said when Danny stood up. "It's not going to do you any good to run away. The chief wants to talk to you, and if you don't speak to him here he'll come after you."

"Okay," Danny agreed sullenly. "I'll go back."

The children went to where the chief stood with Mr. and Mrs. Bobbsey. He held out the geography book. "This yours?" he asked Danny quietly.

Danny shook his head. "I don't know anything about it," he insisted.

"But it has your name in it!" Bert exclaimed.

"What if it has?" Danny snarled.

"I told you it was found by our boathouse," Bert said.

Danny looked worried but said, "You probably took the book and put it in your old boathouse yourself!"

"Watch what you're saying, young man!" Mr. Bobbsey said sternly.

Under questioning by the fire chief, Danny finally admitted that he and Jack Westley had been in the Bobbseys' boathouse just before suppertime.

"Where is this other boy?" the chief inquired.

Danny nodded toward a group whose members were watching the proceedings from a distance. When the chief called him, Jack Westley slowly came over.

"What were you two boys doing in that boathouse?" the fire chief asked.

For a few seconds there was no reply. The others waited. Then Danny spoke up defiantly, "We were looking for clues!"

"Clues!" Bert said in amazement. "To what?"

"We thought maybe we could find that old statuette," Danny said. "Jack and I are just as good detectives as you Bobbseys!"

Flossie giggled. "The snake goddess is back in the school museum, Danny!" she exclaimed. "Bert found it this afternoon!"

Danny looked downcast but said nothing. The fire chief turned to Jack. "Did you light any matches while you were in the boathouse?" he asked.

Jack looked at Danny but did not reply. "Tell the truth, boys," the chief advised.

"Maybe we did light one or two," Jack admitted finally. "But we didn't start the fire!"

"It probably hadn't started when you left," the chief explained. "However, if a match landed on that blanket before the flame was completely out, it may have smoldered there. Eventually the blanket set fire to the boathouse!"

Danny and Jack looked frightened. "We—we didn't mean to hurt anything!" Danny stuttered.

"Maybe not," the fire chief acknowledged. "But you're old enough to know that it's dangerous to play with matches! Get in my car over there!"

"Wh—what are you going to do?" Jack asked, his face turning pale.

"I'm going to take you both to your homes and explain to your fathers what has happened.

It's up to them to see that you don't do such a thing again!"

The two downcast boys walked off with the fire chief and were driven away. By this time there were only a few stragglers still prowling around the damaged boathouses.

Officer Murphy came back to the Bobbseys. "I'll take you home if you're ready to leave," he called.

"Thanks very much," Mr. Bobbsey replied. "Then Sam can get gas for my station wagon."

"I'm glad our boats didn't burn up," Flossie declared as she climbed into the back seat with the other three children.

"And I was a real fireman and squirted a real hose!" Freddie said blissfully.

At that moment they heard a loud barking. Then a shaggy white dog jumped out of the bushes and into the glare of the headlights.

Snap!

Officer Murphy slammed on his brakes quickly, and the children tumbled out of the car. Flossie threw her arms around the dog.

"Oh, Snap!" she cried. "I'm so glad to see you!"

Snap pranced around, giving high, excited barks. His fluffy tail wagged so hard that his whole body shook. After he had greeted each of the Bobbseys he ran off into the woods.

"Stop him!" Nan urged. "He's going away again!"

But before Bert could catch him, Snap came back. He was still barking. When Bert went up to pat him, the dog ran toward the woods once more.

By this time Officer Murphy, flashlight in hand, had joined the Bobbseys. "I think he

wants you to follow him," the officer remarked.

"I think so, too!" Nan agreed. "Let's go!"

With the officer in the lead, the group walked into the woods. Snap trotted along ahead of them in a very businesslike manner.

Farther and farther into the woods they went.

"Do you think he really knows where he's taking us?" Mrs. Bobbsey finally asked nervously.

Snap had stopped and was running around in circles, sniffing at the ground. Then he seemed to have found what he wanted. He left the path and struck off toward the lake.

"Where do you suppose he's going?" Nan asked, puzzled.

Just as she spoke, Snap gave a happy bark and bounded forward. A man was seated on a rock by the water, his head in his hands.

"Hello there, Bob!" he said, pulling the dog's ears affectionately. "I'm glad to see you— thought you'd run away again!"

Then he heard the footsteps behind him and jumped up. When he saw the brass buttons on Officer Murphy's uniform in the beam from the flashlight, the man spoke. "I did sleep in that boathouse, officer, but I'm sure I didn't cause the fire!"

Murphy flashed his light on the speaker. The

Bobbseys saw a slender young man with bright blue eyes and reddish hair.

"Red Rankin!" Bert burst out.

The man looked startled. "That's right, son," he said, "but how did you know me?"

"Mr. Hayden at the circus told us about you," Nan explained.

The young man still looked puzzled. Officer Murphy spoke up briskly. "I suggest we all go back to the car and discuss this."

After they had made their way out of the woods, Mr. Bobbsey smiled and said, "Officer, if you can take us all to my house, we can talk there, and you can get back to headquarters."

"I hope the chief doesn't spot me with eight people and a dog in my car!" the officer said with a grin. "But it isn't far, and three of my passengers are small!" Freddie and Flossie giggled. Snap barked.

On the way to the Bobbsey house Red Rankin explained that he had very little money when he had to leave the circus in Lakeport. "I wandered down to that lake and decided I'd spend the nights in one of those boathouses until I could find other work."

He looked upset. "I was very careful not to disturb anything, and I never lighted any matches. I'm sure that fire wasn't my fault!"

"Don't worry, Rankin!" Mr. Bobbsey said kindly. "We know who caused the fire, and it wasn't you!"

"But when did Snap find you?" Freddie put in impatiently.

"Snap?" Red looked confused.

"We named your dog Snap," Bert explained. Then he went on to tell Red Rankin how the shaggy white dog had followed the Bobbseys from the train wreck, and had seemed to want to stay with them.

By this time the police car had reached the Bobbseys' house. As the family walked up to the front porch, Dinah threw open the door.

"Land sakes!" she exclaimed. "I've been worried about you! Is the fire out?"

Then she saw Snap. "Where did you find him?" she asked. "I'm sure glad to see him home again!"

Flossie took their visitor's hand. "This is Mr. Red Rankin," she announced. "Snap belongs to him," she added sadly.

Dinah peered at the man. "Howdy do," she said. "Why you're the man who was here on Saturday looking for work."

Mr. Bobbsey led the way into the living room. "I think we should sit down and talk," he said.

The twins' mother added, "Dinah, will you

please get us something hot to drink? We've been standing out in the chilly night a long time!"

"Yes, ma'am. I sure will!" Dinah bustled out of the room.

Freddie and Flossie followed her to the kitchen. There they breathlessly told the cook about the rescue of the boats, the discovery of Danny Rugg's book by the burned boathouse, and how Snap had suddenly met the Bobbseys and led them to Red Rankin.

"Well, I declare!" Dinah exclaimed. "You all certainly have had an exciting evening!"

The small twins helped Dinah carry in the cups of steaming cocoa and a big plate of cookies. As Mr. Bobbsey took a cup, he addressed Red Rankin.

"Suppose you tell us about yourself," he said kindly.

In a low voice the dog trainer said that after his trick dog had disappeared, he had stayed in Lakeport, hoping to find the dog and rejoin the show.

"But I couldn't locate Bob," he went on, "so I started looking for any kind of work. Then yesterday Bob came running into your boathouse!"

"He knew you were there because you dropped your red handkerchief in our back yard, and he followed your trail!" Flossie said excitedly. "But we couldn't find you!"

"I didn't spend too much time in the boat-house," Red explained with a smile.

"What are your plans now?" Mr. Bobbsey asked. "Will you go back to the circus?"

Red Rankin looked uncertain. He explained that only this afternoon he had found a job with a construction company. "They want to send me to Panama. To tell you the truth, I'm a little tired of circus life and would like to try something else," he ended.

The twins looked at one another in excitement. If Red Rankin was going to Panama, would he take Snap with him?

Mr. Bobbsey had the same idea. "I'd like very much to buy your dog," he said. "The twins have grown very fond of him!"

The young man looked relieved and sad. "Well—Bob and I are old friends and I hate to part with him." The owner glanced at the forlorn faces around him. "However—I'd be glad to let Bob stay in such a good home," he declared finally.

Nan and Bert thanked him quickly. Freddie and Flossie jumped up and clapped their hands while everyone beamed.

"Snap is ours!" Freddie cried. "Whoopee!"

BOBBSEY TWINS
CLASSIC EDITIONS

DATE DUE

SEP 0 7 2010		
MAY 1 1 2011		
JUL 1 6 2011		
AUG 1 2 2011		
JAN 0 4 2012		
AUG 0 2 2012		
SEP 1 0 2012		
NOV 0 5 2012		
GAYLORD		PRINTED IN U.S.A.